Keep It Together, Keiko Carter

DEBBI MICHIKO FLORENCE

Scholastic Press / New York

Library of Congress Cataloging-in-Publication Data

Names: Florence, Debbi Michiko, author.
Title: Keep it together, Keiko Carter / Debbi Michiko Florence.
Description: New York: Scholastic Inc., 2020. | Summary: Keiko, Audrey, and Jenna have always been best friends, and Keiko desperately wants it to stay that way, but now they are starting seventh grade, and everything seems to be changing; Audrey is obsessed with the idea of them all securing boyfriends, but when she and Jenna focus on the same boy their friendship starts to break apart—and then Keiko finds herself attracted to Audrey's brother, Conner (who has generally been cast as the enemy), and suddenly she finds herself having to choose between the two.
Identifiers: LCCN 2019024109 (print) | LCCN 2019024110 (ebook) | ISBN 9781338607550 (ebk) | ISBN 9781338607529 (hardcover)
Subjects: LCSH: Japanese Americans—Juvenile fiction. | Best friends—Juvenile fiction. | Dating (Social customs)—Juvenile fiction. | Friendship—Juvenile fiction. | Choice (Psychology)—Juvenile fiction. | Brothers and sisters—Juvenile fiction. | CYAC: Japanese Americans—Fiction. | Racially mixed people—Fiction. | Best friends—Fiction. | Friendship—Fiction. | Dating (Social customs)—Fiction. | Choice—Fiction. | Brothers and sisters—Fiction.
Classification: LCC PZ7.1.F593 (ebook) | LCC PZ7.1.F593 Ke 2020 (print) | DDC 813.6 [Fic] —dc23
LC record available at https://lccn.loc.gov/2019024109

10 9 8 7 6 5 4 3 2 1   20 21 22 23 24

Printed in the U.S.A.   23
First edition, May 2020

Book design by Stephanie Yang

For Jo Knowles and Cindy Faughnan—
writing partners and dear friends,
you're both better than chocolate

one

Some people think that all chocolate is the same, but they're wrong. Chocolate can be buttery or bittersweet, crumbly or creamy. Some chocolates have undertones of cherry or coffee or vanilla. My friendship with my best friends was like the best high-quality chocolate— sweet and smooth. Or at least it had been. Right now, I wasn't sure, and I just wanted things to get back to normal.

I had a plan all mapped out. Get the three of us together, someplace we all liked. Talk about the good things that had happened this summer. Laugh like best friends, tease each other like best friends. Then, get us excited about the start of seventh grade.

"Audrey, come on!" I rapped on the metal frame of my best friend's front screen door. I knew if I went into the house, it would be even harder to get her to leave with me. I popped a couple of M&M's in my mouth. I felt my shoulders relax as I crunched into the candy shells and the earthy sweetness melted on my tongue.

Minutes later I heard footsteps. I shifted out of the way as Audrey pushed the door open and finally came outside.

"What's the rush, Keiko?" Audrey smoothed her hands over her white shirt, then patted the back pocket of her pink shorts to check for her phone.

"Aren't you excited to see Jenna?" I asked.

Jenna Sakai was our other best friend. Her parents had gotten divorced last year, and her dad had moved to Texas, so for the first time in three years, Jenna had spent the summer away from us.

Audrey's hair, the color of milk chocolate, fell in soft waves over her shoulders. She'd stopped wearing it in a ponytail just last month. "She completely ignored us all summer," Audrey said.

"Not *completely*," I said. The three of us had all started out with good intentions, messaging back and forth, but it got hard keeping it up. Partly because I felt bad telling Jenna every little thing we were doing without her. She had probably spent the summer sitting around her dad's apartment alone while he was at work.

"She stopped texting us," Audrey said, swiping on lip gloss instead of the lip balm she'd been using over the summer. Her lips looked shiny and smelled like strawberries.

"We kind of stopped texting her, too."

Audrey waved her hand. "Jenna stopped first."

"Audrey," I said. "Don't be mad." What I really wanted to say was, *Don't ruin our reunion.*

I walked down the steps first, hoping to get Audrey moving. Over the summer, she'd decided that riding our bikes was childish. We were going to be turning thirteen—Audrey in November and me in February. After two weeks of being stuck at home, we'd begged our parents to let us take the bus. They agreed, but only to and from The Courtyard, the fancy outdoor shopping center, during the day and with advance permission. That first ride was special. Audrey

3

documented every part of our trip, from waiting at the bus stop to sitting together on the hard bus seats, and she snapped a selfie in front of every store we visited. Then she printed up the photos and made me a collage of our day. I had it hanging on my bedroom wall.

Now the bus would be coming in fifteen minutes, and I was worried she was trying to miss it on purpose.

At first it was weird not having Jenna around. We'd always done things as a threesome, riding our bikes around the neighborhood, going to the park for ice cream, playing board games at my house, and watching movies at Audrey's. The first few weeks of this summer, Audrey and I had texted Jenna to try to include her. Audrey even blew up a photo of Jenna's face and put it on a stick, and we took selfies with it wherever we went, like Jenna was still with us. That was so like Audrey to come up with a sweet and clever way to make Jenna feel included. But Jenna's responses were always short, and by July, she'd take a while before answering us. Then in August, she stopped texting us altogether. Audrey had stopped by then, too. She said Jenna was selfish and didn't care about us, but I didn't believe it for a second. Jenna had never really been into constant texting—even before summer—and had zero interest in social media. She was just really different from Audrey. Audrey was Hershey's Kisses and Jenna was more like a small-batch dark chocolate bar.

"Oh great," Audrey said under her breath as she followed me down the porch steps.

Before I could ask her what she meant, I heard the worst sound ever.

"Yo, it's the Pancake Twins!" Conner Lassiter, Audrey's brother, shouted as he and his idiot friends, Doug Nolan and Teddy Chen, walked up the block. They were a year older than us but acted like they were five.

I crossed my arms over my chest, something I did a lot these days. Audrey sped past me and I hurried after her, going the long way to the bus stop. There was no way we wanted to go by the boys on purpose.

"God, they're such brats!" Audrey said. "I can't believe we're going to have to see them at school."

Seventh grade started in just two days. At Pacific

Vista Middle, the sixth graders had a separate building and a different lunch period, so we never had to run into Conner and the Morons last year. But now we'd share both.

"The campus is pretty big," I said. "The chances of bumping into Conner are slim, especially if we figure out where he hangs and then avoid him."

I dropped my arms from my chest, needing to swing them instead to keep up with Audrey. At least now we wouldn't miss the bus. My knees started to ache from stomping on the sidewalk like it was Conner's face. You'd think eighth-grade boys would be more mature. Last year, Doug came up with the nickname the Great Wall of China for Audrey, Jenna, and me, which was super weak, especially since none of us are Chinese. Jenna's Japanese American; I'm half Japanese American; and Audrey is a mix of English, Irish, and French.

When we got on the bus, Audrey kept busy on her phone, texting with her cousin Sylvia, who lived in San Francisco and was in high school. These days, Sylvia seemed to be the expert on everything from fashion to romance.

Three stops later, Audrey and I stepped off the bus

at The Courtyard. We loved coming here to shop and walk around because all the stores were outside between palm trees and flowering plants, fountains, and brick walkways. The only real tragedy was that there were no chocolate shops.

Audrey and I headed to our usual meeting spot by Heart & Seoul, the Korean BBQ food truck. She kept texting while we walked. Ever since she'd gotten her own cell phone at the start of sixth grade, she was constantly on her phone, messaging other people and checking celebrity sites. It had been annoying at first, since I had to wait to get my own phone till my birthday months later, but now I was used to it. I stretched my neck to try to see around the back-to-school-shopping families and teenagers crowding the walkway, dodging shopping bags and ginormous purses.

"There she is!" I said, nudging Audrey.

Jenna stood next to a metal bench by the food truck, her shoulder-length hair now an electric blue, not the black-with-a-pink-streak she'd had in June. The rest of her looked the same, though—faded jeans and Angry Little Asian Girl T-shirt.

When we reached Jenna, I was so excited, I lunged at

her. I caught myself, though, because Jenna wasn't big on emotional displays.

"One hug," she said. Then she surprised me by wrapping her arms around Audrey and me and squeezing. It was over before I could blink, but it was a good sign.

"Whoa," I said, my heart filling with relief and happiness. "You must have really missed us."

Audrey said nothing. I took one look at her mouth closed tight as she stared down at her phone, and my stomach wobbled. Jenna was happy to be with us, but Audrey acted like she'd rather be somewhere else.

"How was Texas?" I asked, filling up the silence. "Different from California, I'll bet."

Jenna sat down on the bench and shrugged. "Different. Yeah." She rummaged in her army-green messenger bag. "I brought back gifts."

Audrey perked up at this. "You did?" She sat down next to Jenna, finally smiling and putting her phone away.

"This is for Keiko." Jenna handed me a chocolate bar.

"Single-bean dark chocolate," I said, reading the label. "From Madagascar! Wow! Thank you!"

Jenna grinned. "Like it would be hard to please you."

Audrey shifted, her hands fluttering, trying to mask her impatience.

Jenna handed Audrey a box. I sat down on the other side of Jenna and watched as Audrey ripped off the top. She gasped and lifted out a sturdy pink metal lockbox. "Awesome!"

"No more hiding your thumb drive in your tampon box," Jenna said.

"That reminds me," Audrey said, pointing at me. "Tell Jenna!"

"I finally got my period, like, two weeks after you left for Texas," I said with some pride. Audrey's had started in the sixth grade. She warned me that it might take a while for it to come regularly. So far, I hadn't had it a second time.

Jenna raised her left eyebrow at me.

"It wasn't something I wanted to text," I said. "Has yours started yet?"

Jenna's cheeks turned pink and she shook her head once. I wasn't sure if that meant she hadn't had it yet or she didn't want to talk about it. Jenna was super private.

"This is great." Audrey opened the lockbox. "I keep

worrying that Mom will have one of her rare but overly thorough cleaning sprees and toss out everything under the bathroom sink."

Audrey had to share a desktop computer with her horrible brother. She journaled all her precious memories and thoughts, and there was no way she would risk having Conner find them and use them against her. So she stored everything on a thumb drive and hid it in a tampon box in the bathroom they shared. It was a truly brilliant hiding place.

"Thanks, Jenna," Audrey said.

Jenna smiled. I nudged Jenna, and she nudged me back.

Relief melted over me. Now *this* was the perfect reunion! The three of us were together again, without any leftover weirdness from being apart. Of course, I would have liked it if we had all spent the summer together, but Audrey and I'd had a really fun time. We'd watched a bunch of movies and talked nonstop about what seventh grade would be like, and Audrey had given me countless manicures. The sharp prick of guilt stabbed me, but I pushed it away. I wanted to bask in this moment. Audrey fiddled with her gift from

Jenna, a smile playing on her lip-glossed mouth, and Jenna and I leaned our shoulders against each other. I didn't want anything to ruin this moment.

"I have something kinda cool to tell you guys," Jenna said.

two

I turned to Jenna, eyes wide. "Oh yeah? What?"

"Wait!" Audrey leapt out in front of us, holding up her hand. "First, the Theme!"

My best friends swiveled to me. Every year, I set up a theme for us. Like the Year of Stickers, when we'd collected and traded stickers in third grade. Last year was Hayao Miyazaki, when we'd watched as many Miyazaki films as we could and collected figurines. I loved *My Neighbor Totoro*, Jenna was all about *Princess Mononoke*, and Audrey was in love with *Kiki's Delivery Service*.

"Well, this year we're turning thirteen," I started.

"We know this," Audrey said.

"Let Keiko finish," Jenna said, missing the glare Audrey threw her.

I cleared my throat. "Now that we're in seventh grade, we can join any clubs and activities we want." As sixth graders, we had only been allowed to do sixth-grade activities. "This year, the Theme is Experience! We will each pick one club, and the rest of us will join. We'll be in three activities together, and more importantly, experience them together! We'll have new adventures!"

"Cool," Jenna said.

"Hold up!" Audrey waved her hands.

Jenna and I looked at Audrey.

"I love your Theme of Experience idea," Audrey said. "And having adventures together. But I know something that's more exciting than clubs and activities."

"What?" I asked.

"Boyfriends!" Audrey pressed her hands to her heart.

I blinked at Audrey, not knowing what to say.

"What kind of theme is that?" Jenna asked. "Besides, Keiko's the one who comes up with our themes, and hers is perfectly good."

Audrey dropped her hands and frowned.

"No, no," I said, standing up next to Audrey. She'd finally warmed back up to Jenna, and I wasn't going to let that change. "That's fine! That's a great theme."

"Oh really?" Jenna asked.

"Just think," I said to Jenna. "All three of us with our first boyfriends. Together!" I was starting to like Audrey's idea. "We could triple date! Imagine getting ready for our dates together, picking out our outfits, and then later rehashing everything. Just like Audrey's magazine articles talk about!"

Audrey looped her arm through mine. "See? Keiko's on board!"

Audrey's always been boy-obsessed. I'd lost count of all the boys she'd crushed on since fifth grade. It wasn't until this summer, though, that I started noticing boys in a way that made me feel jittery inside, like I'd eaten too much chocolate. There had been a super cute guy who worked at the Heart & Seoul food truck this summer. Audrey had asked him where he went to school, saying she wanted to help me get to know him. I had been mortified, then disappointed when he said he was only visiting for the summer from Seattle.

So, the idea of a boyfriend made me feel like melted

chocolate, all gooey and warm. Jenna was going to be resistant. She was the practical one, the unemotional one, the good student. I tensed, waiting for Jenna's protests, but she only shrugged.

"We can still sign up for all the same clubs," I said as a concession.

"The world is our oyster!" Audrey announced, making me laugh. I glanced at Jenna, who quirked her lips in a small smile.

Last year in the language arts class Audrey and I were in together, our teacher campaigned against clichés so enthusiastically that Audrey started using them on purpose. But not in front of our teacher.

"Now that the Theme is decided, let's move on to more important things! What did you do all summer?" I asked Jenna.

"Not much."

"You missed out," Audrey said quickly. "Conner and his friends went camping a couple of times, so Keiko and I had the whole house to ourselves. Four nights in a row of sleepovers twice this summer! Like we were sisters." Audrey smiled at me. "I would trade Conner in for you any day."

I grinned. "And now we're all together again! This will be our best year yet!"

"Ooooh!" Audrey exclaimed, tugging us along with her up the walkway. "I just got a great idea! Let's go look at dresses."

"I'm good for clothes," Jenna said.

Audrey stared at Jenna. "*You* went shopping?"

Of the three of us, Jenna was the least interested in fashion.

"Dad couldn't stop spending money on me," Jenna said, lifting her messenger bag over her shoulder. "As if new clothes and a laptop were going to replace having him at home."

It was rare for Jenna to talk about her parents' divorce, and when she did, I never knew what to say. I didn't like seeing her so sad.

"You got a new laptop, *too*?" Audrey's voice was soaked in envy. She had an unlimited budget on most things, but that didn't include getting her own computer.

"Well, it doesn't matter, because this isn't for school. Not really." Audrey snapped her fingers. "Follow me."

Jenna and I trailed after Audrey, who stopped in front of a little boutique called Whispers. In the window, headless mannequins wore sequined gowns that looked more for our moms than for us.

"Come on," Audrey said with a grin as she stepped into the store.

A little bell tinkled, and a blast of chilled air hit us as we walked in the door. Audrey started going through a rack of dresses.

I turned to Jenna, who was shifting her bag from shoulder to shoulder. "So, you wanted to tell us something?"

Jenna smiled and nodded.

"What do you think of *these*?" Audrey asked, holding up several dresses that looked way too fancy for anything I'd ever go to. One dress had sparkly beads and looked heavy.

"Um, they're nice?" I had no clue what Audrey's plan was.

"Come on. Let's try these on!" Audrey led us to the biggest dressing room after getting a nod from the saleslady at the counter.

"What are we doing here?" I asked as she closed the

curtain behind us. "Please don't tell me this is what you think we should be wearing in seventh grade."

"Two words," Audrey said. "Fall Ball!"

PV Middle had two dances a year for the seventh and eighth graders, Fall Ball and Spring Fling. Both were fund-raisers for the school, raising money for things like library books or basketball uniforms.

"Let me get this straight," I said. "These are Fall Ball dresses we're trying on?"

Audrey nodded.

"Shouldn't we get dates first?" I gave Jenna a side-long glance, expecting her to back me up, but instead, she was looking at the two dresses closest to her.

"Yes! Totally!" Audrey said. "This is part of the plan, Cake!"

"Don't call me that," I said, frowning.

"I gave you that nickname!"

"In the first grade." I used to love my nickname. Audrey shortened Keiko to Cake because she said I was sweet, but last year, her stupid brother ruined it when he started calling me things like Flatty Cake, Mud Cake, and Betty Crocker.

"Okay, you're right," Audrey said. "Shedding our

childish ways! All for the great life as teenagers we're about to have. When we *get* boyfriends, we're going to go to Fall Ball!"

"But what if we don't get boyfriends immediately?" I asked. "Shouldn't we have a plan? Like maybe in September, we could scope out possibilities. Then in October and November, get to know a possible boy-friend. And if all goes well, an actual boyfriend by the end of the year. Maybe we should shoot for Spring Fling, instead." That sounded way more manageable.

"I'm not wasting the entire year without a boyfriend," Audrey said. "Just try the dresses on, Keiko. For fun!"

I turned to Jenna for support, but she was already tugging off her shirt and jeans.

"Those sports bras only make you look flatter," Audrey said to Jenna. She probably would have gone on, but Jenna's look silenced her.

I faced the wall as I slipped off my hoodie and whipped on the closest dress in one fluid motion. I'd had a lot of practice in the locker room. I tried to zip the dress, but the zipper wouldn't go up all the way. I looked in the mirror. The light blue contrasted nicely with my dark brown hair. I kind of liked the sparkly beads after all. Even in a store for grown-ups, Audrey had good taste. But the spaghetti straps made me feel naked. Even with the snug fit, when I leaned over, the front of the dress gaped to reveal not only my twelve-dollar girls' department bra, but the bra gaped, too, and I got a good flash of my own skin.

I put my hand over the front. Jenna was already out of the first dress, something black and slinky, and zipping up the second. But the sweetheart neckline did nothing for her athletic figure. Her eyes met mine in the mirror, and her lips twitched. I held in a giggle.

Audrey turned to us, dressed in a pale pink dress that clung to her. She looked like a ballerina.

"Oh, Audrey," I said. "That's pretty on you. How much is it?"

Audrey glanced at the price tag and gasped. "Five hundred!"

"Dollars?" Jenna squeaked. She slowly removed her dress, like she was afraid she'd rip it. I didn't blame her. I followed her lead, peeling mine off in slow motion.

As I hung up the dress, I heard Audrey sniffle.

"Don't worry," I said. "We have plenty of time. First, we get boyfriends, then we'll find the perfect dresses for the dance."

We left Whispers and their overpriced, too-fancy dresses and walked to the big fountain with the comfy lounge chairs. Audrey and I sat on a wicker couch under a green-and-blue umbrella. But as soon as my butt hit the navy-striped cushion, I regretted our choice. Jenna stood by three orange chairs with her arms crossed.

I waved her over and said, "I want to sit in the shade."

I scooted over and Jenna sat down next to me. It was a little tight. In the past, the three of us had always sat in those three chairs right in front of the fountain. But this summer Audrey and I started sitting on this couch, and I now realized that it didn't fit three comfortably. I hoped Audrey wouldn't complain. I didn't want Jenna to feel left out.

"Did you get to see any movies this summer?" I asked Jenna, moving my arm carefully onto my lap so I didn't keep jabbing her with my elbow. It was hard to turn my head to face her, so all three of us stared out at the walkway.

I felt Jenna shrug. "Not really. You guys?"

Audrey leaned forward and made a little more room. "We saw a ton, especially if you count the movies we watched at my house," Audrey said to Jenna. "You know how Cake, sorry, I mean Keiko, was all into those boring old black-and-white movies? I got her to watch better retro movies, from the eighties."

"Like what?" Jenna asked.

"Movies by some guy named John Hughes. *The Breakfast Club* was totally great, but I think Keiko liked *Pretty in Pink*."

"Never heard of them," Jenna said quietly.

"We can watch them again with you," I said. "Or watch others. We didn't see all of them."

I still loved those old black-and-white movies, even if Audrey said they were boring. But I also liked the ones we'd watched over the summer. Audrey was right. *Pretty in Pink* was the best. Andie, the main character, had two boys who liked her: her best friend, Duckie, who was kind of weird but funny, and this rich guy Blane, who hung out in a snobby clique. After Blane snubbed her and hurt her feelings because of his stupid friends, he realized he'd made a mistake. It was romantic how at the school dance, he apologized and told her he loved her. They had the perfect kiss at the end of the movie.

That's what I wanted. If Audrey's plan worked out this year, I wanted a romantic boyfriend and a perfect first kiss.

three

We watched shoppers pass us for a while, basking in a comfortable silence, the kind that best friends have. The scent of sunscreen and roses floated by on the warm air.

"So," Audrey said, moving to perch on a low table in front of the couch, "what kind of boyfriend do you want?"

I envisioned a combination of Blane and Duckie from *Pretty in Pink*. "Romantic, funny, sweet, easy to talk to, and cute," I said. "Basically, perfect."

"Perfect is an impossible standard," Jenna said, tugging a strand of her blue hair.

"Okay, maybe not perfect," I said. "All I need is some-one who's the opposite of Conner."

"Keiko can have whatever she wants," Audrey said to Jenna. Then she turned to me. "You have to go after your happiness. Don't let anyone talk you out of it."

I glanced at Jenna, who scowled at Audrey. Quickly, I switched the focus off me. "How about you, Audrey?" I asked. "What are you looking for?"

"I already know who I want to be my boyfriend."

"Already?" I asked. I shouldn't have been surprised. Audrey always had a crush going. But her goal of get-ting a boyfriend and wanting to go to the dance was definitely new.

She paused and flashed a teasing smile. Jenna wrapped an unraveling thread from her T-shirt around her index finger. I nodded at Audrey.

"Elliot Oxford," she announced.

Jenna yanked the thread so hard it came off and made a tiny hole in the hem of her shirt.

"Really?" I asked.

"What?" Audrey sounded annoyed. "You think he's out of my league?"

I shook my head. "He doesn't seem your type. I mean,

25

isn't he kind of brainy?" I turned to Jenna, who was on the honors track. "No offense."

"Do you know him?" Jenna asked Audrey.

"Not really, but we had PE together last year and I saw him a couple of weeks ago when I was grocery shopping with my mom. He's cute! In a nerdy way."

I glanced at Jenna, who was staring at the hole in her shirt. I could sympathize. I didn't want to get involved in another one of Audrey's crushes, either. Last year, Audrey had us stalking Nick Vandrow's locker. He never noticed us, or if he did, he ignored us. And then a couple of months later when she liked Jason Hatami, we hung out at his dad's hardware store on the weekends, just in case Jason stopped by. He never did. There were only so many times we could browse hammers. Who knew there were so many kinds?

"I have to get home," Jenna said.

"We haven't had anything to eat yet," I said.

Jenna stood and shouldered her bag.

"You taking the bus?" I asked.

"I rode my bike." Jenna pointed to the front parking lot where the bike racks were. "Wait. You guys took the bus?"

"Mom and Dad finally said it was okay." When Jenna glanced down at her feet and frowned, I added, "I meant to tell you."

"We would have if you hadn't stopped texting us," Audrey said.

"I didn't stop," Jenna said. "You guys did."

"It was only for the last couple of weeks," I said really fast. "We can catch up on everything now!"

"I told my mom I'd go shopping for school supplies with her. I'll see you guys later." Jenna started walking away. I chased after her.

"Wait! Jenna!" I said when I caught up with her. "You said you had something to tell us."

She glanced over my shoulder as Audrey joined us. "Maybe later."

We watched Jenna unlock her bike and ride away. I elbowed Audrey.

"What?" She raised her hands.

"She was stuck in Texas. We probably made her feel bad by telling her about our week-long sleepovers and all the movies we saw." I slumped. I was a horrible friend. How could I have been so insensitive? "We have to make things right."

"Look, school starts in two days," Audrey said. "We'll be hanging out all the time again. Everything will be back to normal. Better than normal."

I hoped she was right. Audrey and I have been friends since first grade, while Jenna and I met in second grade. Our dads used to work at the same company. When our parents would go out, they'd pool a babysitter for me, my sister, and Jenna. It wasn't until Jenna's family moved into our school district and Jenna started going to our school in the third grade that Jenna and Audrey finally met. Jenna had been the new girl, but because of me she immediately had friends, me and Audrey.

Shopping with Audrey was fun. She helped me pick out two cute shirts and a pair of light blue pants. I usually only ever wore jeans, but Audrey encouraged me to try something new. After we were shopped out, I went straight home. I dumped my shopping bags in my closet and sat down at my desk with Jenna's gift. I loved a good chocolate bar. I unwrapped it, broke off a square, and slid it into my mouth. As it melted on my tongue, I closed my eyes. I kept seeing Jenna's hurt face when she'd realized we'd started taking the bus and hadn't told her.

I should have kept texting with her even when she didn't always answer. I should have made sure she knew she was missed.

That earlier twinge of guilt pinched me. I'd missed Jenna for sure. Mom had always said that threesomes were hard, but our friendship never felt hard. And it wasn't. But last year, I started noticing how different Audrey and Jenna were from each other. They didn't fight or anything, but they didn't always agree. Jenna wasn't an enthusiastic fan of things Audrey liked to do, like practicing yoga, taking online quizzes, and complaining about Conner. Plus Audrey, who had always been interested in fashion, was even more obsessed now. And Audrey didn't love to talk about Jenna's various environmental causes and latest articles on her favorite news sites. This past summer when it was just Audrey and me, I didn't have to worry about keeping the peace between them. I loved Audrey and Jenna equally, but they probably wouldn't have become friends without me. I was the one who overlapped them, the intersection of two circles of a Venn diagram.

But as much as summer with Audrey had been fun

and relaxing, I loved our threesome. Audrey and Jenna were my second family. We balanced one another, like the ingredients of chocolate.

I would make sure Jenna knew that I wished she had been home with us. I'd make it up to her. I'd make sure she knew she was still important to us. To me.

I needed a new plan. Once we joined clubs, I was sure things would click back into place. Maybe we could start a new tradition. I'd come up with something. That made me feel better. I ate another square of chocolate.

I looked at my Totoro clock. I hoped Mom would get home early from the children's museum. I wanted to tell her how happy I was that Jenna was back. Ever since Mom had gotten promoted in June from part-time education associate to director of education, she was hardly ever home.

I went downstairs to the kitchen. This past summer, I'd spent most of my time at Audrey's. Her parents worked a lot of hours, and Audrey liked having the house to ourselves. Conner had spent most of his time at Doug's, fortunately. But I usually saw my family for dinner. Dad had gotten a Japanese cookbook and tried out almost all the recipes. Mom was thrilled and said it reminded her of the meals she'd had growing up. My favorite had been tonkatsu, fried panko-crusted pork cutlets with a sweet thick sauce. My stomach rumbled with the memory.

The back door opened and I turned with a smile. But it wasn't Mom.

"Hey," I said to my little sister, Macy.

She grinned.

"Had fun at Claire's?" Macy's best friend since forever.

Macy pushed her bangs off her forehead. Her hair was a lighter shade of brown than mine.

"Yeah," Macy said. "We decided we're going to join the drama club."

"When did Sandpiper Elementary get a drama club?" They hadn't had one when I left two years ago.

"We have a new fifth grade teacher, Mr. Diggs. He used to write and act in plays before he became a teacher," Macy said, smiling. "I'm going to try out for a part."

"Wow, really? You want to be an actor?"

"What?" she said with a frown. "You don't think I'd be any good?"

"I didn't say that. I'm just surprised. I mean, you have to audition, right?" What if she didn't make it? She might be devastated.

"Yeah," Macy said. "Auditions are this week."

"You should talk to Mom. See if it's okay."

Macy gave me a look. "Well, maybe I won't join. It was just something Claire and I were thinking of doing together. It's our last year of elementary school."

That reminded me of how I wanted to join clubs with Audrey and Jenna. I mean, we were still doing that, but now we had this whole other Theme going on. Boyfriends. I really wanted to talk to Mom and get her advice on all this.

"What time is Mom coming home?" Macy asked, practically reading my thoughts.

"It's Monday, so probably around five, same time as Dad."

"It's weird with Mom working full-time," Macy said. "I kind of miss her. We won't have snack time after school. Everything's changing." She pulled a strand of hair into her mouth, a nervous habit I thought she'd broken years ago.

"No it isn't. It's just a little different, but nothing's

32

changing." I didn't like that Mom was away so much, but I didn't like Macy being upset, either.

Macy spit her hair out and it stuck to her chin. Gross. "That *is* change," she said. "If it's different, it's not the same."

I climbed the stairs and went back into my room. Macy acted like I had a problem with change. I mean, look at everything I was embracing. Audrey came up with the Theme for the first time ever. And we were going to try to get boyfriends and go to a dance. I wasn't afraid of change.

Just as long as everything else stayed the same.

four

The next day, the day before school started, I went to Audrey's house. We texted Jenna to invite her over, but she never answered.

"Typical," Audrey said, sitting on the couch in the den.

"I'm sure she's busy. She just got home from being away," I said, plopping down next to her.

"She's acting like she's too busy for *us*!" Audrey played with a silver bangle on her wrist.

"Let her get settled back in at home," I said. "It's going to be fine." It *had* to be fine. It had felt off with Jenna away all summer, like we weren't quite whole.

I was counting on our threesome getting back to normal. We belonged together.

Audrey leaned her head back against the couch. "You're right. I just want this year to be great, you know? My cousin Sylvia's life changed in middle school. She got really popular and was busy in all these activities, and now she's a cheerleader in high school with a boyfriend who is on the varsity basketball team."

"That's what you want? To be popular?" My throat got tight. I didn't want to lose Audrey to a clique of girls I didn't know.

"No, silly," Audrey said, smiling at me. "I don't need to be popular or anything. I just want us to have fun. I don't want to be exactly how we were in elementary school, though. I want to do teenager things!"

"Like?"

"Get a boyfriend, wear makeup, go to parties and dances, meet new people." Audrey waved a hand at me. "Not replace you and Jenna, but just have, you know, a bigger circle of friends."

That didn't make me feel better. It wasn't that I didn't want other friends, but I didn't need them. Our trio worked. I wasn't sure what would happen if we added anyone new. I didn't want to talk about this anymore.

"Feel like watching a movie?" I asked.

Audrey strolled over to the DVD cabinet. Her parents had been collecting DVDs for decades.

"Old-school viewing for old movies," Audrey said, holding up the DVD for *Ferris Bueller's Day Off.* We'd watched it three times over the summer.

When Jenna had watched movies with us, the three of us would sit on the floor with our backs against the couch, Audrey in the middle holding a bowl of popcorn on her lap. Over the summer, Audrey and I started sitting on opposite ends of the couch, our feet meeting in the middle. We settled in our spots as the movie started. Audrey and I laughed in all the same places. My worries over Audrey replacing me and Jenna faded. We had too much history, the three of us. We'd be fine.

An hour and forty minutes later, we waited as the credits rolled and at the same time as Ferris Bueller, Audrey and I shouted, "You're still here? It's over!"

We laughed.

Audrey stood and stretched her arms up. "I'm hungry."

I followed her to the kitchen, where she dug around in the pantry while I sat at the counter.

"Look what I got for you." Audrey set a Trader Joe's bag in front of me.

I reached in and one by one removed a bag of cocoa nibs, cinnamon sticks, allspice, and black peppercorns.

"Wow! You know all the ingredients?" I was amazed. I made a spicy hot chocolate that I loved, but Audrey didn't.

"You've made it enough." Audrey put the ingredients back into the pantry. "These are yours and you can make your hot chocolate anytime you're here."

"Thanks!"

Audrey nabbed a bag of spicy dill pickle potato chips and opened it, pushing the bag between us on the counter. We grabbed handfuls and munched. In July, we'd seen the chips at the corner market and been totally grossed out. Who wanted potato chips that tasted like pickles? I'd dared Audrey to eat them. So she bought them and tried one and liked it! I had, too. It became our snack of choice. I wondered if Jenna would like them.

"This was kind of the summer of snacks," I said, dusting chip crumbs from my fingers.

Audrey popped open a Diet Coke and nodded. "Right? It's like we tried everything. Those fried plantains from the Cuban place, and then the green tea donuts at the coffee shop. You loved those!"

"They were good," I said, remembering. "Oh! Guess what? There's a new bubble tea place opening today. They're giving out free samples. Let's go check them out!"

Audrey groaned. "Ew! No thanks."

"Oh come on! You know I love bubble tea."

"Those balls of tapioca are like chewing snot."

At that moment, Conner and his dog, Lumpy, walked through the kitchen. Conner wore a Lakers basketball jersey and shorts, and a red dog leash dangled from his hand. Lumpy danced alongside Conner, excited for a walk. I ran my hand along Lumpy's silky black fur as he passed.

"Ha! You should like that then," Conner said to Audrey. "You and snot, perfect match."

"Shut up!" Audrey said, scooting away from Conner and Lumpy.

Conner laughed and walked out the front door with his dog.

"Ughhhhh!" Audrey clenched her hands into fists. "I hate him!"

"Let's go to my house for dinner," I said, wanting Audrey back in a good mood. "My dad is supposed to get home early for our night-before-school dinner. You can come. And we'll text Jenna and invite her, too." My parents never minded when Macy or I brought friends home for dinner.

As we walked to my house, my phone buzzed with an answer from Jenna.

"Well?" Audrey asked, peering over my shoulder.

I shook my head. "She's having dinner with her mom."

Audrey made a small sound.

"It's nice she gets to spend time with her mom," I said.

"It is," Audrey conceded. "At least you both have moms who want to hang out with you." Her parents ran a photography shop and spent all their time there, which made sense since it was their business. But that meant Conner and Audrey were alone a lot. When we were all in elementary school, Conner and Audrey, and later Jenna, used to come to my house after school. Mom wouldn't let us watch TV, so we played Mom's old board games like Life, Sorry!, and Payday. That had been fun.

"Your mom likes hanging out with you! She takes you shopping."

Audrey didn't say anything.

When we got to my house, no one was home yet.

"Come on," Audrey said. "I'll do your nails for school." Over the summer, Audrey had convinced me to buy five different colors of nail polish.

In my room, she pulled out the bottles from my desk drawer, then settled me on my bed. She grabbed a book from my shelf, placed a tissue over it, and pulled my right hand on top of it.

"Shiny New or Minty Fresh?" Audrey held up a metallic silver polish and a neon green one.

"How about Beach Walk?" I pointed to the taupe bottle.

"Boring!" Audrey exclaimed. "Come on, Keiko. Be adventurous. This is seventh grade!"

I picked First Crush, a sparkly pink that Audrey

said would look great on me. "Who comes up with these nail polish color names anyway?" I asked, holding still while she brushed a coat onto my thumbnail.

"I would love that job!" Audrey said. "Hey, did Jenna ever share her class schedule with you?"

"No." Our schedules had arrived a few weeks ago. Audrey and I had texted Jenna so that all three of us could open them at once, but that was around the time that Jenna had stopped responding. So Audrey and I had opened ours at her house. We ended up with only one class together, language arts. How unfair was that? We'd had the same classes all through elementary school, and we always sat next to each other. In sixth grade, we'd had most of our core classes together. We didn't share many with Jenna.

Audrey closed the cap on the bottle while I blew gently on my drying nails. I held them up and smiled. They didn't look bad.

Dad walked into my room. "There you are!" He ruffled my hair like I was still ten. I didn't mind. "Nice nails," he said.

"Hi, Mr. Carter," Audrey said, smiling.

"Always great to see you here, Audrey! I hope you're staying for dinner."

Audrey nodded.

"Come down and keep me company," Dad said.

We followed him down the stairs and leaned on the kitchen counter. Dad grabbed the pizza stone from the cabinet. I turned on some tunes, Dad's usual retro stuff, and he and I sang along to the music as he prepped a pizza and made salad. Even Audrey, who usually didn't like Dad's taste in music, joined in on "We Are the Champions" by Queen. Dad loved to cook. Before Mom got the promotion, the whole family would prep dinner together, with Dad doing most of the work. Macy and I mostly goofed off, but it was fun hanging out in the kitchen with Mom and Dad, even when they got silly and danced around to the music.

Macy strolled in as we were pulling out the piping-hot pizza from the oven.

"Where's Mom?" she asked.

"Yeah, where *is* Mom?" I chimed in. She should have been home by now.

Dad checked his phone. "Oh, she says she has a late meeting and to go ahead and eat without her." Dad handed Macy napkins to put on the table. "She'll eat later."

"But it's night-before-school dinner," I said. "We always eat together as a family before the first day of school." My stomach clenched, but it wasn't from hunger.

"She's writing that grant, remember?" Dad said.

Audrey and I sat down at the table, and I glanced at Mom's empty chair. It looked wrong. "What time will she be home?"

"I don't know," Dad said, "but probably very late."

I frowned, but when I saw Macy watching me, I pasted on a smile.

Dad cut the pizza and placed it in the center of the table. I let everyone pick their slices before I took one for myself. Usually, on night-before-school dinner, I couldn't get a word in as we all talked over one another. Mom always led the conversations by asking a million questions about our hopes for the new school year. But tonight, Dad checked his phone for work emails, and Audrey and Macy talked about some TV show I didn't watch. I missed Mom's questions.

I missed Mom.

five

The next day, I was thrilled to see Jenna in first period
social studies. As I slid into the seat behind her, I saw
that she had already arranged her colored pens in a
neat row above her notebook.

"Where were you yesterday? Audrey and I wanted to
hang out with you," I said.

"Mom put together a special mother-daughter day.
I think she missed me."

"Yeah, we *all* missed you. What did you do?"

"We went to the zoo! I think she wishes I were still
ten. But it was fun. Mom was relaxed for once. And she
only made three mean comments about Dad."

That was progress. Jenna had nearly fallen apart during her parents' really nasty divorce. They'd stabbed each other with their lawyers' sharpened tongues, not seeing that Jenna was getting slashed, too. I'd never forget how Audrey and I had been at Jenna's one evening, before the divorce, and we'd all overheard normally polite Mrs. Sakai scream curse words at Jenna's dad. That was the last time Jenna had us over.

All through the second half of fifth grade, Mom had invited Jenna to our house for dinner and sometimes to sleep over. Jenna and I would sit in my room after dinner, and she'd tell me how awful it was to hear her parents fighting all the time. Once, she'd said she wished they'd hurry and get a divorce, yet when it was actually happening, she kind of shut down. But that could also have been because of Audrey.

Audrey hadn't been happy that Jenna was spending so much time at my house, so I started inviting her over, too. At first Audrey tried to be a good friend, listening to Jenna and offering advice, but Jenna didn't much care for that. Then Audrey tried to cheer her up by bringing snacks or funny books, but that hadn't worked, either. In the end, Audrey complained about how boring it was hanging out with us, so I brought out board games and we stopped talking about Jenna's troubles.

I snagged the remaining half bar of chocolate Jenna had given me from my backpack and broke off a square for each of us.

"What do you think?" She tossed it into her mouth, hardly tasting it before she chewed and swallowed.

"It's excellent," I said. "Thanks again!" I let the smooth, slightly bittersweet chocolate melt a little on my tongue as the class started filling up. "Soooo," I said. "You had something to tell us?"

"I did." Jenna twirled a purple pen between her fingers.

"But now you don't?"

"Promise not to tell Audrey?"

"We can't *not* tell Audrey." I shifted in my chair. "Is it about her?"

"Kind of."

"But you said it was good news, right?"

Jenna gave me a tight smile.

Before I could ask anything else, our social studies teacher, Mr. Jay, loped in, balancing a stack of folders and a cup of coffee. Jenna went into straight-A-student mode: facing forward, sitting ramrod straight, pen in her hand and ready to take notes. I knew our conversation was over, at least for now. Mr. Jay spent most of class talking about what to expect from the semester, including a final project involving ancient Rome or something. I couldn't really concentrate, because I was too hung up on what Jenna's good news could be—and why she didn't want to share it with Audrey. We'd never had secrets from each other before.

At the end of the period, Jenna ran off to her next class. The only other class I had with Jenna, it turned out, was PE, so I'd have to wait till last period to find out more. There was lunch, but Audrey would be there, and now I knew she wouldn't talk about it in front of Audrey.

I walked into language arts knowing Audrey would be saving a seat for me. When I saw her smiling face, I was suddenly relieved Jenna hadn't told me her mysterious secret. I was a horrible liar. I didn't want to be disloyal to Audrey. I'd find out the secret and then make sure Jenna told Audrey. Best friends didn't keep secrets from each other.

"Can you do me a favor?" Audrey asked as we moved our chairs into a circle. It seemed that Ms. McQueen was big on discussion groups.

"Sure," I said, sitting down next to her.

"Actually, it's a favor for Conner."

"Forget it." The last thing I wanted to do was help Audrey's annoying brother.

Audrey dropped her voice to a whisper as Ms. McQueen passed out copies of *The Outsiders*, the first book we would be reading. "Please? Conner's camping this weekend, and Mom and Dad are going to a photography workshop on Friday night. Can you please take care of his disgusting dog? You and Jenna can stay over."

The disgusting dog, as Audrey put it, was Lumpy, the Labrador mix Conner had found two years ago. For some reason, Audrey hated Lumpy almost as much as she hated her brother.

"Sure," I said. I loved that dog, even if he had a moron for an owner. I'd think of it as a favor for Audrey and a bonus for me.

The happy thought of time with Lumpy and a sleepover at Audrey's carried me through my next two classes.

At the start of lunch, the three of us met at the cafeteria. It was overwhelming. The school had received some big donation and renovated over the summer. The cafeteria now looked more like a mini mall food court than a school lunchroom.

The lines were super long, but we finally, finally got our trays of food, pushed our way back outside, and searched for a place to eat.

"This is a critical choice," Audrey said. "Wherever we choose now will be where we eat for the rest of middle school."

In sixth grade, we'd had to eat by the cafeteria. Now we could eat anywhere on campus. We followed Audrey to a picnic table under a magnolia tree.

"Not sure this is the best place," Jenna said. She pointed at a few white splotches on the tabletop. "Looks like birds perch in the branches above."

Audrey screeched and leapt away from the table.

I looked around. "There!" I nodded toward a grassy spot next to the main building. "Let's sit there!"

We sat down, Jenna on my left, Audrey on my right. Both of them started eating; neither said a word.

"Hey," I said. "Remember Disneyland?"

The three of us had gone over the summer, right before Jenna had left for Texas. We'd had fun the whole day, riding the rides, laughing, and talking. Jenna's mom had been happy reading a book on a shaded bench the entire day, letting us run around the park on our own as long as we checked in every few hours.

"That was fun," Audrey said. "At least until Keiko got sick on the Teacups."

"I didn't get sick!"

"No," Jenna said, "but you were an amazing shade of green."

"Almost neon," Audrey said.

Jenna and Audrey shared a laugh, and I didn't care at all that it was at my expense.

"At least I didn't puke," I said.

"Good thing you didn't have that extra hot dog after all," Audrey said. "And remember that guy who tried to cut in front of us at Space Mountain?"

"What a total loser," Jenna said.

"You told him to get back in line!" Audrey squealed, still scandalized. "I can't believe you said something!"

I nodded. That guy had to have been fourteen at least, but Jenna would not let him pass.

"He was really mad," Audrey said.

"Then the other people wouldn't let him cut, either." Jenna laughed.

That was better. I picked up my burger, but then the sight of Audrey's brother and his idiot friends sauntering our way made me lose my appetite.

"Hey, look! It's Tawdry, Fruit Cake, and Jester!" Conner said.

"Get bent!" Audrey snapped.

Conner and the Morons snickered as they passed us, nudging one another like the idiots they were. The hamburger bun crumbled in my grip.

"Jester?" Jenna laughed. "That's the best he can do with my name?"

"God," Audrey said. "I can't wait till they go camping this weekend. I hope Conner gets eaten by a bear!"

"Don't let him get to you," Jenna said.

"Easy for you to say," Audrey said. "You don't live with him!"

Stupid Conner. He was the absolute worst! He annoyed me for sure, but he really got under Audrey's skin. Whenever he put her in a foul mood, which was often, it was hard to get her out of it. One thing I knew for sure: If I wanted any chance of this year being the best ever, I had to figure out a way to avoid Conner at all costs.

six

"Can't you tell both of us what your big secret is?" I asked as I stood in line with Jenna to do basketball drills. I hated PE, but Jenna was a natural at sports.

"It's not a *big* secret," she said.

"So, tell us both." I caught the ball thrown my way. I dribbled and, surprisingly, made a layup. I basked in a brief moment of glory while Jenna caught the rebound and passed the ball to the next person in my line.

"I'll tell you if you promise not to say anything to Audrey," she said as we headed to the back of the line.

I couldn't do that. How could I keep a secret from

Audrey? My insides churned like I'd eaten cheap chocolate. "She's our best friend, too."

A shrill whistle cut through the air. Coach Yang's voice boomed across the courts. "Carter! Sakai! Stop your gabfest and get back to your drills!"

Probably not a great thing that Coach knew our names already. I tried to concentrate on dribbling and shooting, but I was filled with worry about how to stay loyal to Audrey while finding out Jenna's secret.

Audrey had always put me first. When we were in the fourth grade, we planned to be partners for the school-wide science fair. I had really wanted to do a project with animals, and Audrey, who loved fashion even back then, wanted to test which fabrics were easiest to dye. Her idea was more specific, so I agreed to go along with it.

Two days later, when we were supposed to be picking out fabrics to dye, I was looking through a stack of dog books on her kitchen table.

"Whose are these?" I asked.

"Conner's," Audrey said, cutting out a square from her dad's old cotton shirt. "He's doing his project on canine sense of smell."

"That sounds awesome!"

Audrey looked up from her fabric square. "Our dad's friend is letting Conner test different smells out on his cocker spaniel."

I didn't say anything else and dutifully cut out a square from Audrey's mom's silk shirt. I found out later that Audrey had not had permission to cut it up. Her mom got really mad at her.

The next day Audrey talked our teacher into letting me work with Conner on his project. This was a big deal for Audrey—I knew how badly she wanted us to be partners.

Conner and I had come in third place. And even though Audrey didn't get any recognition for her project, she celebrated my win as if it were hers, too. We went out for ice cream and she made me a special congratulations card that I still have today, tucked in a box of cherished things under my bed.

"Good work, Carter," Coach called out to me at the end of the period.

I have never ever had a PE teacher say anything positive about me in class. I grinned all the way to the locker room.

After I changed back into my street clothes, I met Jenna at her gym locker just as she was tying her shoes.

"Tell me before we go to the library," I said. The secret was making me prickly. I took out the last square of the chocolate bar and broke it in half, giving Jenna the bigger piece. I'd figure out how to get Jenna to tell Audrey later.

"Okay, okay." Jenna shoved the chocolate in her mouth and devoured it. She took a deep breath and let the words come out in a cocoa-fueled rush. "Elliot Oxford and I started emailing and texting my last week in Texas, and . . . I think I like him."

"Wait, what?" A slow smile spread across my face, matching Jenna's grin. "That's so awesome!"

Jenna nodded, and then her grin faded.

"Oh," I said, wishing I had more chocolate. "Audrey."

"She's not going to take it well," Jenna said, propping her feet up on the bench.

"But it's not like she's going out with him," I said. "Just tell her."

Jenna shook her head.

"Why not?"

"She's going to get mad." Jenna scowled.

"No, she won't. I mean, she might be upset at first, but she'll be happy for you!"

"Remember that time when we all entered that online contest to come up with a caption for a photo?" Jenna retied her shoelaces. "You and Audrey consulted with each other, but I went ahead and sent mine in without sharing it. Not because I didn't want to tell you guys, but because I came up with it in the middle of the night and sent it off."

I sighed. "Yeah, and you won an honorable mention, while Audrey and I didn't win anything." I hadn't cared about not winning. I'd been happy for Jenna. Besides, she'd shared her prize with us: a giant bag of every kind of candy our ten-year-old brains could imagine. But Audrey had acted like Jenna had betrayed us. She didn't talk to Jenna for a week.

"Anyway," Jenna said, standing up, "there's nothing to tell. It's not like we're boyfriend and girlfriend or anything. I don't even know if he likes me that way."

"Right, so just tell Audrey that. She'll get it." I stood up, hitching my backpack on my shoulder. "Hey, is that why you stopped texting us?"

Jenna shook her head. "You guys hardly texted me in

August. So, it wasn't like *I* was the one who stopped. It was like we ran out of things to say. You guys were having all kinds of fun without me, and I wasn't doing anything interesting. Elliot and I only started emailing because he had a question about the summer reading list our sixth-grade honors language arts teacher gave us. And we just kept talking … about other stuff. And then we started texting."

I nodded.

"There isn't really anything to say about Elliot. I mean, I was going to tell you guys about him, but then Audrey said she liked him."

"It's okay! But I think you have to tell her," I said. Audrey might be disappointed, but like I said to Jenna, it wasn't like she and Elliot were a thing. It was better to get this over with. "Rip that Band-Aid off."

Jenna shrugged. "You're right."

When we got to the library, Audrey was already there. I thought she'd be annoyed that we were late, but when Jenna and I sat down, Audrey flashed us a mysterious smile.

"What's up? You look like you're about to burst," I said.

Audrey giggled. "You can tell?" She leaned toward us, grabbed our hands, and squeezed. "I'm on the Fall Ball committee!"

"Wow," I said. "I thought we were all going to sign up for the same clubs?"

"So? Join!" Audrey spread her arms wide. "We can do this together!"

The thing was, I didn't want to be on the dance committee. My idea of joining whatever club the others chose might not have been great after all. "Maybe we can join something else together."

"Sure! Whatever. But this will get us the inside scoop on the dance. I'll know the theme and when the tickets will go on sale ahead of time. Now all we have to do is get boyfriends!" Audrey turned to me. "Did you pick a guy?"

"What? No."

"Don't tell me there wasn't one cute guy in any of your classes who interested you even a little bit."

I glanced at Jenna, as this would be the perfect time for her to say something about Elliot, but she was busy taking out her ten billion pens.

"You're too picky, Keiko," Audrey said in a low

voice. "There has to be some guy who doesn't disgust you."

"I'm not picky," I said. I *did* want a boyfriend, but I didn't want it to be just anyone. I wanted that flipping-heart feeling, that rush of emotion when we were together. I knew better than to expect a *Pretty in Pink* romance, but I wasn't going to lower my standards, either.

"Okay," Audrey said in a soothing tone. "At least narrow your field. Pick, say, three guys, who might be possible candidates."

I nudged Jenna under the table with my toe, but she was now busy pulling out her notebooks.

"How about Sam from our history class last year? Or Logan from math! Is he in any of your classes?"

I shook my head. Sam was a nose-picker. Or at least I saw him pick his nose in the fourth grade. That was a hard image to forget. And last year, Logan called Colette a fat cow. Not to her face, but still!

"Logan is cute," Audrey said.

"Then you take him." I wasn't going to settle. Somewhere out there was the perfect guy for me.

Audrey laughed. "I already have a boyfriend in mind, remember?"

How could I forget? I gave Jenna a sharp look, but she managed to avoid my eyes. I was just about to nudge her with my foot again when Audrey turned to Jenna. "We need to work on you," she said. "Who do you like?"

I held my breath.

"I joined the newspaper," Jenna said.

"Fabulous," Audrey said. "Joining clubs and organizations are great ways to meet boys!"

"Wait, what?" I turned to Jenna. "When?"

"Today. You know I like to write." Jenna caught my look and said, "You guys can join, too."

Audrey laughed. "I don't think so! Writing for fun? That's so not my thing."

Jenna shrugged and looked at me.

"I don't know," I said. "Maybe." I couldn't believe Audrey and Jenna had gone off and joined clubs without telling me. We were supposed to be doing things together.

"Oh my God, it's him!" Audrey grabbed my arm.

I started to turn around, but Audrey squeezed my arm. "Don't look! Don't be obvious!"

I didn't need to turn to know who it was. Jenna's

eyes bulged out in panic as she shoved her books into her bag. Her pens rolled onto the carpeted floor, but she didn't bother picking them up.

"Where are you going?" Audrey whispered.

"I just remembered I have a doctor's appointment." Jenna grabbed her things, walked a wide path around Elliot, and made it out the door without him seeing her. When I turned back to Audrey, she was staring wistfully at him. Oh boy.

This could get very ugly.

seven

By Friday, Jenna, Audrey, and I had fallen into a nice routine, and things felt normal again. Jenna got to school super early, since her mom dropped her off before work, and liked going straight to class to study before school started. So I'd meet Audrey at her locker in the morning, and we'd chat on our way to class. Then at lunch, Jenna and I would find each other in the cafeteria line to buy food. Audrey usually brought hers and would wait for us at the grassy area we now called ours. The only dark moments were when Conner and the Morons showed up toward the end of every lunch period with their drive-by insults.

We had a good thing going, studying in the library together after school and gossiping about everyone in our grade, just like we always had. Our sleepover at Audrey's was tonight and I didn't want to upset the balance, so I had kept Jenna's secret to myself. But I knew Jenna had to tell Audrey about Elliot. And she had to tell her tonight. It was the right thing to do.

After lunch, I had pre-algebra and plopped into my chair hoping it would pass quickly so I could start my weekend. I reached into the side pocket of my backpack, pulled out a small gold box, grabbed the closest truffle, and popped it into my mouth. Dad had brought the chocolates home from a client and given them to me.

Just as I bit into the crisp chocolate shell, a gorgeous guy walked into the classroom. For the first time in my life, I swallowed chocolate without tasting.

"Class?" Our teacher, Mr. Fordiani, immediately got our attention. A new kid, especially a *cute* new kid, always got attention. "This is Gregor Whitman. He just moved here from Michigan."

Whitman...like the chocolate company! I wasn't sure if it was the spark of recognition at Gregor's name or the fact that he had caramel-colored hair and eyes the color of rich ganache that had me staring. He wore dark jeans and a cream sweater that was too warm for a Southern California fall. Instead of Converse or Vans, he had on dark brown hiking boots. He didn't dress at all like the boys in Pacific Vista. Very interesting!

The only empty desk was right behind me. Gregor smiled as he passed, and I felt him settle into his seat.

"Keiko, can you please share your notes with Gregor?" said Mr. Fordiani, my new favorite teacher. "Gregor, you've only missed two days, so it will be easy to catch up."

For the rest of the class, I could hardly concentrate. I kept looking at the clock to see how many minutes were left until the end of the period so I could turn and face him. I glanced at the clock again. I swear it was broken. The second hand was moving in slow motion. I willed it to move faster.

By the time the bell finally rang, I'd almost passed out from the exertion of trying to make time speed up. I gathered my notes, hoping to face Gregor Whitman without an audience. No such luck. Kimmie Chin and Nicole Morgan stopped at the desk behind me.

"Hi, Gregor," Nicole said, all perky. "What a cool name."

"Thanks," he said. His voice was smooth like melted chocolate.

"What class do you have next? We can show you where it is," Nicole said.

I turned around and got a close-up of just how adorable Gregor was. His hair fell in a slight wave above his eyes, and he had long lashes and a full lower lip. I flopped my notes onto his desk.

"You can return them to me on Monday," I said, a little under my breath. I got up and left before waiting to see if he'd acknowledge me. I wished I had Nicole and Kimmie's confidence and had offered to walk him to his next class. My cheeks burned just imagining doing that.

After PE, where Coach put me and Jenna on separate basketball courts for scrimmages, Jenna took off for her after-school newspaper meeting and I headed to the library to study with Audrey.

"Look," Audrey said as soon as I sat down. "I'm the only one who's picked a boyfriend. You and Jenna need to pick someone soon or you won't have enough time before the dance tickets go on sale."

"I think I know who I want to go with," I said softly.

Audrey grinned. "Finally! Tell me! Who is it?"

I glanced around, just in case anyone was lurking. But we were the only ones in the library so early in the semester. "He's new. In my math class." I pressed my hands against my cheeks, trying to hide my blush. "And he's super cute."

"Oh! That's so great, Keiko! I'm happy for you!" Audrey gushed.

"Don't be too happy," I said. "I doubt anything will happen. He probably won't even notice me."

Audrey's eyes flicked to something over my shoulder.

"Keeko?" A newly familiar smooth voice came from behind me. Gregor stepped up to our table.

"Hi," I squeaked.

He glanced at Audrey and flashed her a smile. "Am I interrupting?" he asked.

"Of course not," Audrey said.

"Gregor, this is Audrey Lassiter, one of my best friends. Audrey, Gregor." At least my voice went back to normal. My heart was pounding so far up my throat I was surprised it didn't come flying out of my mouth.

"Hi!" Audrey said brightly. "Come sit!"

I flashed her a look. What if he didn't want to sit? What if he was only passing through, just being polite? I was thrilled he'd even stopped. And he knew my name! Never mind that he said it wrong.

As soon as Gregor sat down next to me, Audrey popped up and started gathering her books.

"Where do you think you're going?" I asked.

"I forgot I have to meet Tricia to talk about dance committee stuff."

When Audrey lied, her nose flared. Not that Gregor would know this. Audrey ignored my glare and smiled at Gregor. "The school holds fund-raising dances twice a year. I'm on the Fall Ball committee, so I have all the inside scoop! Tickets will go on sale in a month."

I was surprised my face didn't burst into flames. Could she be any more obvious? I was going to kill her.

"Anyway, I'm sure you two can get along without me. See you later!"

Yep. I was seriously going to kill her.

Gregor pulled out his math book and flipped it open

to where my notes were neatly folded in half between the pages. "Thanks for sharing."

"No problem," I said, taking my paper back from him.

"Do you have time to review yesterday's assignment? I want to make sure to do it even though Mr. Fordiani didn't say I needed to."

"Sure." Who knew I'd be grateful to talk about math?

He scooted his chair closer to mine. Oh. My. God! I couldn't believe Gregor was sitting right next to me! Even though we weren't touching, I could feel his body heat radiating from him. But I tried to focus on yesterday's lesson.

"It was mostly review from last year," I said, too loudly. I lowered my voice and shoved my notebook toward him. "Here."

"Thanks."

I didn't dare look at him. He was so close. If I leaned slightly to my left, my knee would touch his leg.

He slid my notes back to me. "You're right. It's just review. Do you want to do our homework now? Or do you have to be somewhere?"

"No, I don't have plans." I could have been offered a

tour of the Godiva factory and I'd totally skip it to do math homework with Gregor Whitman.

As we both started the assignment, I wondered if I should be making conversation or if he wanted to focus on his homework. I didn't want to be annoying.

I wished we were sitting across from each other so that I could at least glance at him from under my hair. I changed my mind about that when, suddenly, Gregor's arm bumped mine as he erased something on his paper. It felt like an electric jolt flamed a trail from my elbow to my face. I held still, hoping he'd bump me again. He did! Twice! The second time, he mumbled his apologies. Okay, so maybe Audrey did me a favor by leaving. Maybe I wouldn't kill her. Maybe I'd thank her.

After we double-checked our answers with each other, we gathered our books. I headed to my locker, expecting Gregor to peel off, but he kept walking with me. This is what I'd dreamed about, walking through the school with a cute boy. Maybe Gregor would become my very first boyfriend. We'd go to the dance together. Maybe he'd kiss me. I snuck a glance at him, and he smiled, which made a grin burst out on my face.

"So, you're from Michigan?" I asked. "What's that like?"

"It's cool," he said.

Silence descended.

"The weather must be different there than in California." I wanted to smack myself. *Really, Keiko? The weather?* Why couldn't I think of something interesting to say?

"Yeah. It's going to feel weird not having snow in the winter."

"Sure." I sighed. I got lost in the thought of snow, and we walked the rest of the way in silence.

When we made it to my locker, I twirled the dial on the lock. Gregor leaned against the wall, watching me. I messed up my combination twice before finally opening the door.

"So, what kind of name is Keeko?" he asked.

"It's Japanese," I said as I slid my math book into my locker.

"Oh. But you speak English without an accent."

I glanced at him to see if he was kidding around. Only Gregor wasn't laughing. He just stood there waiting for my answer.

"I'm American. I was born here. So were my parents," I said.

"Ah. So that's why you have a regular last name." He shook his head. "I mean, an American last name."

"My dad's white. My mom's Japanese American."

"Cool."

I tossed my books into my locker. I guess it made sense that he wanted to know about my name. It meant he was interested in me. Or in my name, at least. Keiko *was* unique.

"Do you like chocolate?" I asked.

"Sure."

I handed him one of my milk chocolate truffles and held my breath as he chewed thoughtfully, trying not to stare as he swallowed.

"Tasty." His smile made me feel like a puddle of ganache.

Before I could respond, a grating voice cut through the air. "What is that splotch on the wall?"

Conner and the Morons walked toward us. "Oh!" Conner smacked his forehead. Not as hard as I wanted to smack it. "It's Cake Splatter."

The guys laughed. It wasn't even that funny or clever!

Why didn't they just disappear? The campus was big enough that I shouldn't have to run into them during lunch *and* after school.

Gregor stayed silent long after the guys passed. I had to say something.

"That was Audrey's brother and his friends. Their brains run on empty most of the time."

"They seem like jerks."

"That's an understatement," I said, grateful he didn't mention Conner's insult.

"You should ignore them."

"I try."

"Where do you eat lunch?"

The abrupt subject change surprised me. "What?"

He smiled. "Lunch? Where do you eat it? Can I crash your party?"

"Oh!" He wanted to eat lunch with me? "Sure. Of course. You can totally join us. It's just me, Audrey, and our friend Jenna. You haven't met her yet."

"That's great. So, where do you eat?"

I blushed. "Oh, um, right." Gregor laughed. He had a very nice laugh. "The big grassy area next to the main building. Across from the walkway."

"Nice. I'll see you there on Monday."

"If you want, I can show you around the cafeteria."

"Sounds good."

I waved as Gregor strolled out of the building. He had a very nice walk. I smiled. Maybe soon he'd be walking with me to classes...or even walking me home.

eight

When I got home, I tossed my backpack on the floor.
Dad was at the kitchen counter, pulling out spice jars
from the rack. I ran over and hugged him. My joy was
bubbling over.

"Hey," Dad said, turning to me. "That's a nice greeting. Good day?"

I nodded, smiling so hard my cheeks hurt. "You're
home early."

"I just got here," he said. "Thought I'd make a big
dinner for us."

"Oh," I said, feeling bad. "I texted Mom. I'm going to
Audrey's for a sleepover. I should have told you, too."

"Ah, okay. More food for the rest of us, then." Dad pulled out a cutting board and started chopping onions and carrots.

I was just about to turn on the music for him when I heard a car pulling into our driveway. Dad and I exchanged smiles. He wiped his hands on a towel as Mom dashed in the back door, her hair pulled back with a headband and her black cotton skirt swirling around her knees.

"Mom!" I gave her a hug. Now my day was perfect. I could catch Mom up on what was going on and maybe even tell her about Gregor.

She squeezed me and moved on to give Dad a kiss.

"Sorry," she said, breathlessly. "Ignore me! I'm not really here."

"I'm making dinner," Dad said.

Mom shook her head as she rummaged through a pile of papers on the back counter. One thing I learned early was to never move or straighten Mom's papers. They looked like messy piles, but to her they were organized messy piles.

"I can't. I have a meeting in"—she glanced at the

kitchen clock—"thirty minutes. I left my notes for the Carlson School project here."

"Mom," I said, "you'll never guess what's going on with Audrey and Jenna."

"Found it!" Mom held up a blue folder. She leaned over to kiss my cheek. "I'll eat something at the meeting."

And then she was gone. Mom sure was busier than I thought she'd be. I hated not being able to tell her what was going on in my life. And not knowing when I'd get the chance.

"Well, at least we got to see her briefly," Dad said as I frowned. "Don't worry, honey, it's temporary. As soon as she's done with the grant proposal, she'll be home in the evenings again."

"You and Macy will have a feast tonight," I said.

"Oh, I forgot," Dad said, putting a spice jar back on the rack. "Macy is sleeping at Claire's tonight."

Dad dumped the chopped veggies from the cutting board into a big baggie. "I can eat leftovers and catch up on some reading. A little downtime sounds great."

"Are you sure?" I asked.

Dad laughed and reached out to rub the crease between my eyes. "Stop worrying so much, Keiko. I can take care of myself. I'm a big boy."

I went upstairs to tell Macy to have fun at Claire's, but when I got there, the whole floor seemed empty. I checked the bathroom, but she wasn't there. I knocked on her bedroom door, and when no one answered, I let myself in, wondering where she was. Then I heard the front door close, and moments later she walked into her room.

"Hey," she said, "why are you in my room?"

"I was just going to say to have fun at Claire's," I said, narrowing my eyes at her. "Where were you?"

Macy ignored me and tossed clothes into her overnight bag, then hefted it onto her shoulder. "Claire's mom is picking me up. I'm waiting outside." She pushed past me and headed downstairs.

That was weird behavior for Macy. Where had she been after school and why was she avoiding answering me? I'd need to get her to tell me later.

Jenna, Audrey, and I fell into our usual routine, making nachos the way we had many times before in Audrey's kitchen. Jenna ducked under Audrey's arm as she grabbed a mixing bowl and avocados while Audrey took ingredients out of her refrigerator.

I shredded cheese. Jenna made her famous guacamole. Audrey chopped tomatoes for salsa. No store-bought, premade stuff for us. Well, except for the tortilla chips. We weren't allowed to use the oven or stove when Audrey's parents weren't home, which was most of the time, so we had to stick to using the microwave.

We mixed and chopped while Audrey told us all about the Fall Ball committee. "We're voting on a theme next week. I suggested Tropical Paradise. I hope it wins! We can have flower garlands and fruity drinks with those paper umbrellas. You guys should totally join," she said.

Neither Jenna nor I said anything, but Audrey didn't notice as she told us about each of the girls on the committee. "Tricia is the nicest and Addie has the best ideas."

Conner's dog padded into the kitchen as the microwave beeped, signaling that our nachos were ready. Audrey almost tripped over him as she carried the salsa to the table.

"Ugh," Audrey said. "Stupid dog."

I squatted down to pet Lumpy, who wagged his tail so hard it smacked into Audrey's legs.

"Oh my God!" she said, scooting out of range. "That hurts!"

"It can't hurt that bad," Jenna said, taking the chips with melted cheese out of the microwave. She put the platter on the table.

I nuzzled Lumpy, feeling bad for him. A wagging tail was a good thing. Lumpy was happy. Dogs are almost always happy. That's one of the things that makes them so great.

"Ew, Keiko," Audrey said. "Now your hands are all doggy."

I stopped myself from rolling my eyes and went to the sink to wash my hands. When I sat down at the table, Jenna poured water into three glasses as Audrey dealt out napkins. My heart melted as I watched them exchange smiles when they sat down at the same time. I raised my water glass. "Here's to us, the three amigas! Friends forever!"

Jenna and Audrey touched their glasses to mine. "Friends forever," they said together.

Audrey scooped guac onto a chip heavy with melted cheese and took a bite. "Mmm. Heaven on earth. Magically delicious!"

We laughed.

"That last one is not a cliché," Jenna said.

"Eh, retro commercial jingle. Close enough." Audrey giggled.

We chowed down on our nachos, stuffing ourselves full.

"It was horrible not having you around this summer, Jenna," I said.

"It was horrible not being here. Next year, I hope I won't have to spend the entire summer at my dad's. But I do want to see him."

"I guess we have to learn to share you," I said.

"Sharing's overrated." Audrey snagged the last chip.

Speaking of sharing, I snuck a glob of cheese to Lumpy under the table.

After we cleaned up, Audrey led us to her room. Jenna and I froze in the doorway. Hanging on the far wall was a big handmade banner with "Fall Ball" scrawled across it. Fake flowers in red plastic cups decorated Audrey's matching white dresser, nightstand, and desk.

"What is this?" Jenna held on to the doorframe.

"Surprise!" Audrey spun. "I thought it would get us into the right spirit!"

"The dance is weeks away," I said.

Jenna looked dazed.

"C'mon, guys," Audrey said. "This is supposed to be exciting! Fun!"

"We don't even have boyfriends yet. It just feels like a lot of pressure." I stepped into her room and picked up a plastic cup.

Jenna hung back in the doorway.

"Come in already," Audrey said to her. "We have so much to plan!"

Jenna dragged herself an inch into the room and leaned against the doorframe.

"Now, Cake..." Audrey began. "How close are you to getting Gregor to ask you out?"

Jenna snapped her head toward me. "Gregor? Who's Gregor?"

"He's the new guy Keiko likes. He studied with her today at the library."

I was miles and miles away from Gregor ever asking me out. I tried to grin, but I'm sure it came out more like a grimace. "I think we need to slow down. Maybe follow a plan." I wanted to enjoy the ride, not race to the finish line.

Audrey turned to Jenna. "You're the only holdout. Pick someone and then the three of us can bag our boys before the dance tickets go on sale."

I sat down on Audrey's bed while Jenna still stood silently at the door to Audrey's room.

"What's wrong with you guys?" Audrey asked.

"Nothing," I said, giving Jenna a look. This was it. Time to come clean.

Jenna clenched her jaw. "Audrey, I have to—"

"I understand," Audrey interrupted. "Your parents' divorce was the worst. It's probably put you off relationships. But just because your parents' marriage imploded doesn't mean you can't be happy with a boy."

I held my breath. We never brought up Jenna's parents' divorce.

"You know," Audrey went on, "we can help you. Maybe if you change your wardrobe. You could be really cute if you wore the right clothes. Then guys would notice you."

"I'd rather have a guy notice me for my brains," Jenna said, finally stalking across the room and sitting down next to me. "Or at least have things in common with me."

Audrey nodded so hard her hair flipped around. "Yes! That's the spirit, Jenna!"

I nudged Jenna.

"Promise you'll at least try," Audrey pleaded. "Don't rain on our parade."

"I'm not keeping you guys from doing anything," Jenna said, her voice gravelly and rough.

"Aren't you? You've been so quiet about it, it's like you're mad we want boyfriends."

"That's not it at all." Jenna crossed her arms.

I didn't want them to fight, so I leapt up between them. "I'm going to ask Gregor to the dance. Audrey, give me some advice. Now!"

Jenna stood up, too. "That's an excellent idea. Why should we sit around waiting to be asked? I'll do it, too!"

"Wait, Jenna," Audrey said. "There's someone you want to ask to the dance? That's great! Why didn't you say something?"

Jenna sat down again.

"Tell us!" Audrey said, smiling. "Who is it?"

"Oh, never mind," Jenna said.

"Don't be embarrassed. We won't make fun of you. Cake, help me make her spill the beans."

I have always been a horrible liar. I tried to think of something to say.

Audrey wrinkled her nose as she studied me. She turned to look at Jenna, who was staring at her feet. Audrey swirled back on me. "*You* know?" Audrey's voice went up a whole octave like it always did when she got upset. I tried to swallow, but it felt like a giant marshmallow was stuck in my throat. "*You* know who Jenna likes! Why would she tell you and not me?"

"You knew who Keiko liked before me," Jenna said.

Audrey took a breath. "Right, okay. You two have classes together; we don't. It makes sense. Things slipped through the cracks."

That she used a cliché was a good sign.

"So, tell me now," Audrey said. "Who's the lucky guy?"

I held my breath as Jenna whispered, "Elliot Oxford."

Nobody moved. Nobody breathed. Seconds ticked by.

"What did you say?" Audrey asked, a bit too calmly.

"I'm sorry," Jenna said. "I mean, I'm not sorry I like him, but that you do, too."

Audrey blinked. "Well," she said to Jenna, "you'll have to pick someone else. I have dibs. I called him first."

"He's not a donut," Jenna said.

"Whatever." Audrey waved her hand. "Just pick someone else."

"That's not right," Jenna said.

"I already said I liked him! You don't get to steal him!"

"I'm not stealing him," Jenna said gently.

"Exactly! Because you're going to pick someone else."

"Jenna and Elliot already know each other," I said. "They're friends."

"Because they were on the honors track together last year? So what? That doesn't mean anything."

"We texted each other at the end of summer. Talking about school and other stuff," Jenna said.

Audrey stepped back, like Jenna had pushed her. "You *texted* him?" Audrey sounded like she was accusing Jenna of murder.

"Audrey," I said, wanting to calm her down.

She spun on me. "You kept this from me! How could you? Friends don't keep secrets!"

"Don't be mad at Keiko," Jenna said. "It's not her fault. I only told her on Wednesday. And don't be mad at me, either. It's not like I did this on purpose."

"You broke the code," Audrey said.

"What code?"

"You don't poach your girlfriend's boyfriend! Never ever ever!" Audrey said.

"I'm not stealing him from you. We're not even together. And neither are you!"

"So back off!"

My shirt stuck to my back with sweat. I couldn't think of one thing to say or do to stop this train wreck.

"If you don't, you're not a true friend," Audrey said.

"We don't need to fight over this," Jenna said. "I'm just telling you that I like him, too. That's all!"

"That's not all! Stop talking to him. Don't text him anymore! Don't go near him!"

"That's not going to happen," Jenna said. "We're on the newspaper together."

"So that's why you joined!" Audrey shouted.

Jenna rolled her shoulders back. "You know I love to

write. You know I want to be an author or a journalist someday!"

"Maybe we should take a breather," I said. "We need to calm down and discuss this. But first let's take a break. We'll be in the living room."

As I grabbed Jenna's hand to pull her into the hallway, Audrey pointed at Jenna.

"There's nothing to discuss!" Audrey started to cry. "Either she backs off or she's not our friend anymore!"

nine

"I'm going home," Jenna announced when we got to the living room.

"You can't leave now!"

"She doesn't want us here."

"She's upset and hurt. Let her cry it out, and we can talk about it." As much as I hated conflict, I hated lack of resolution even more.

Jenna shook her head. "This isn't going to blow over in one night. She's being stubborn. I didn't do anything wrong!"

"I know, I know."

"I didn't steal Elliot."

"Of course you didn't. She just needs to calm down. Then she'll come around."

"I can't believe she's acting like this!" Jenna grabbed her duffel bag.

"Don't go," I said. "If you leave, Audrey will think you don't care."

"She already thinks that."

"So prove her wrong."

"By letting her have Elliot?"

"No, I mean, obviously, you're friends with him already. He probably likes you back." I smiled at her.

Jenna's lips tugged upward. "Maybe."

"Audrey will realize you didn't do this to hurt her. She'll forgive you for not telling us earlier. She's just surprised and upset."

"She'll hate me forever." Jenna whipped out her phone and texted furiously.

"No, she won't. Just give her time."

"I think she's going to need more time than just one night, but I'll swing back in the morning." Jenna hitched her duffel bag over her shoulder and snagged her sleeping bag. "My mom's on her way."

I sighed.

As soon as Jenna's mom picked her up, I took Lumpy for a walk around the block. The sky was streaked with pinks and lavenders as the sun set, but the sight didn't cheer me. Jenna and Audrey's fight made me feel sick to my stomach. Audrey had never been this upset before, at least not at one of us. All I wanted was for things to be like they'd always been. We were only into the first week of seventh grade, and everything was changing.

I was so lost in thought that I stopped walking. Instead of tugging on his leash, Lumpy sat down and looked at me, his tongue hanging out.

"You're a good boy," I said, squatting down to hug him. Lumpy leaned his muzzle on my shoulder, and I stroked his smooth fur. At least I had Lumpy for company tonight. Dogs are less complicated than people. They love you no matter what. They never ignore you or judge you or make fun of you.

Lumpy wagged his tail, and pretty soon I felt up to walking back to the house.

When we returned, I got fresh water for the dog and tiptoed to Audrey's room.

I tapped on her door. "Audrey?"

No response. I knocked a little harder, but not too hard. Maybe she was sleeping.

"Go! Away!"

Oops. Or maybe not.

It was early, but I didn't feel like staying up by myself. The couch in the living room was off-limits and only for Mr. and Mrs. Lassiter's rare client meetings at home, and the couch in the den was way uncomfortable. The thought of facing Audrey while she was angry was more uncomfortable, even if she would let me in the room. I wasn't going to give up like Jenna, though. I'd stay and wait for Audrey to cool off.

Lumpy nudged past me in the hall and trotted into Conner's room. I thought about it. Conner wasn't going to be home till Sunday. Did I dare? The idea of sitting on his bed grossed me out, but I could throw my sleeping bag on top of it.

Lumpy was squeezed under Conner's desk but came out to greet me when I stepped into the room with all my stuff and shut the door behind me. I turned on the light on the nightstand and dropped my sleeping bag on the bed, surveying the space.

I hadn't been in Conner's room in more than a year.

He'd painted the walls the color of sand. Gone were the T-ball trophies on his dresser. In their place were stacks of books on dog training and dog behavior, and pamphlets on veterinary colleges. I'd always known Conner loved Lumpy and dogs in general, but this serious interest kind of blew me away.

I went back to the neatly made bed. Conner used to have a basketball-themed bedspread, but that was long ago. The summer before he started middle school, before he turned into pond scum, he got a forest-green quilt. The one other thing that remained the same was the retro movie poster of *Casablanca* over his bed.

Two years ago, Conner and I went on a classic movie binge. *Casablanca, Guess Who's Coming to Dinner, Breakfast at Tiffany's*. Audrey watched that last one with us. She'd loved it, but I hadn't. Audrey wanted to watch it again, but I refused. I hated the Asian character played by a white man. It was totally stereotyped and wrong. His squinted eyes and fake accent were insulting. Audrey told me I was being too sensitive.

"Cake, you're overreacting," she had said, laughing. "It's not like anyone sees *you* that way! You don't have to feel so offended!"

"I *do* feel offended," I'd said, my eyes filling with angry tears.

"It is pretty insulting," Conner said.

Audrey scoffed. "You can't feel insulted. You're white!"

"Don't be stupid," Conner said. "We're not watching it again. Cake's right, it's offensive."

Audrey had been quiet for the rest of the day but later said that it was weird that Conner had taken my side. I hadn't thought so then, but in retrospect, yeah, it was weird, because the Conner of today would have made fun of me.

I unrolled my sleeping bag on the bed and changed into baggy sweatpants and an oversize T-shirt with M&M's candy printed on the front. When I crawled into my sleeping bag, Lumpy hopped up next to me and nuzzled a wet nose against my cheek. This was a bonus. Audrey never let Lumpy sleep in her room. I turned out the light and snuggled up to Lumpy.

The next thing I knew, I was waking up fuzzy-headed. It took me a few seconds to remember where I was. Conner's digital clock glowed 1:15. I squinted in the dark room. Lumpy hopped off the bed as the door opened and shut with a soft click. He greeted Audrey, and she leaned over and gave him a hug.

Wait. Since when did Audrey hug the dog?

I switched on the light and gasped. Conner raised an eyebrow at me.

"What are you doing here?" I asked.

"I could ask you the same thing." Conner straightened. "You have a fight with Audrey?"

"Something like that." It was none of his business. I sat up and rubbed my eyes. "I'll go sleep in the den."

Conner shook his head. He'd let his hair grow out, and a chunk of it fell into his eyes. "Nah. I'll crash on the couch. You're already here. You can stay."

I paused. "I thought you went camping."

"Teddy's dad's car broke down halfway there."

Conner looked tired. Probably why he wasn't insulting me. Lumpy leapt back on the bed next to me.

"He likes you," Conner said. "And you like him."

I hugged Lumpy, and his tail thumped on the bed. "He's the best."

Conner crossed the room and sat down on the corner of the bed. He reached over and scratched Lumpy behind his ears. Lumpy rested against Conner. I felt a twinge of envy. I wished I had a dog.

"I saw your books," I said. "Are you thinking of vet school?"

Conner smiled. Something I hadn't seen except as a sneer lately. "Yeah. It's kind of a dream right now. I have to get good grades."

"Wow."

"Wow?"

"I don't know," I said. "I guess I never thought of you being serious about anything." I clapped my hand over my mouth. Oops. Must learn to think before speaking. Just when we were getting along, I probably ruined the truce, short-lived as it was.

Conner surprised me by laughing. "I guess I deserved that."

My mouth opened, but no words came out.

The silence drew out and I was suddenly aware that I was in my PJs, on Conner's bed, in his room with him.

Conner stood abruptly and crossed over to his desk, a more comfortable distance away.

"I've been a jerk," he said.

"Pretty much." Couldn't argue with that at all. He'd

been obnoxious and mean for more than a year. "What happened? We used to be friends."

"Emphasis on *used to be*."

"Right. Used to be. Thanks to your immature name-calling."

"You think that's where it started?"

We glared at each other until Lumpy whined.

"Right. Whatever."

Normally I'd shoot back another weak retort, but this time I held my tongue. Maybe it was because it was late and dark, or because Audrey was mad and Jenna had bailed, or because having Lumpy next to me gave me a shot of courage, but I didn't let anger blast out of my mouth. I took a breath. "Why?" I asked. "What happened between us?"

Conner pulled out his desk chair and straddled it. "You made a choice," he said, sitting down.

"A choice?"

"Yeah. We were friends. We hung out, all of us, together. But then Audrey got all possessive and weird."

"Oh yeah." Conner and I had often teamed up against Audrey and Jenna when we played board games, and although they won trivia (Audrey) and word games

(Jenna), Conner and I had more fun, laughing and making up silly rules to amuse ourselves. I think Audrey would rather have lost the games than watch me and Conner have so much fun together.

He stared at the carpet. "Audrey told me to stop hanging out with you guys."

"She did?"

"And then she told you to choose, and you made your choice."

It had been during a game of Monopoly at my house. We'd brought Jenna in on the board games in third grade. And the tradition carried on even after we got older and Conner and Audrey could stay at their house alone.

During that particular game, two years ago, Conner and I had been losing, so he suggested pooling our efforts. Audrey called foul. Conner argued that it was fair. They started yelling at each other, and Audrey flipped the game board over onto the floor. Jenna and I had stood up in shock.

Then Audrey said to me, "Conner or me. Who are you going to be friends with? Because I'm never hanging out with my brother again!"

I thought it would pass, but it didn't. Audrey proved she could hold a grudge like no one else. I blinked at Conner. "You've been mad all this time because I picked my best friend? And you thought retaliating by calling us horrible and hurtful names would fix things?"

"I was angry," he said.

"Yeah, but I didn't mean to hurt you. You do and say things to hurt me on purpose."

Conner looked at me for so long that I squirmed and buried my face in Lumpy's fur. I hadn't meant to say all those things. Lack of sleep—that's why I blurted what I felt.

"You're right," Conner said, making me snap my head back up.

I couldn't help adding, "And while we're at it, Doug calling us the Great Wall of China is racist."

Conner hunched his shoulders. "Yeah, I told him to cut that out. I'm sorry, okay?"

I must have been dreaming. Conner was apologizing. "Okay," I said. "But it's probably going to take Audrey a long time to forgive you."

Conner stood up, his arm muscles taut. "I'm not talking about Audrey. I'm not sorry about her at all."

"You're mad at her for something else?"

Conner ignored me and walked backward to the door. "You okay with Lumpy in here? He likes being in here."

"Sure," I murmured as he slipped out the door.

It took me a long time to get back to sleep.

ten

When I woke up the next morning, the door was open and Lumpy was gone. I slid out of my sleeping bag and checked the hall. Audrey's door was still closed. I stared at it, wishing I could just walk in and pretend the fight had never happened. I didn't know why I was afraid. Audrey's my best friend. I should have been able to talk with her. Should.

I went to the kitchen instead. My skin prickled with the morning chill as I grabbed my hot chocolate ingredients out of the pantry. Audrey's kind gesture of buying them for me felt miles away in the past. Her parents had come in late and left a note on the counter saying they were sleeping in.

I put a pan on the stove and dry toasted the cacao nibs, tingeing the air with the earthy scent I loved. Then I dumped the nibs into a bowl and added spices to toast in the same pan. The kitchen warmed up, and the smoky scent of chili wrapped around me like a blanket.

I turned off the stove and squatted to rummage through the cabinet for the coffee grinder. It wasn't in its usual place. I pushed a food processor to the side. I shoved my arm far into the cabinet. Lumpy trotted over to me and licked my face.

I laughed and put my free hand up. "No fair, I can't defend myself," I said, trying to dodge his tongue.

"Are you making your awesome hot chocolate?" Conner's voice startled me, and I bolted up, banging the edge of the counter.

I rubbed my shoulder, then froze as he walked into the kitchen with rumpled bed head and Lumpy's leash dangling from his hand. Conner wore faded jeans and a wrinkled emerald-green T-shirt, the same clothes he'd had on during our middle-of-the-night conversation.

I ducked backed down to continue my search for the grinder. It was weird having Conner talk to me like he did before he'd turned into a jerk. I distracted myself from that thought by making a lot of noise, moving pots and pans until I finally found the grinder shoved behind the blender. Lumpy trotted away and I wondered if Conner had left.

I leapt back up, holding the grinder above my head like it was a trophy. But then I saw Conner standing right across from me on the other side of the counter, and I nearly toppled backward. *Keep it together*, I thought to myself as I set the grinder down between us.

Conner smiled and I think I smiled back.

"Did you take Lumpy for a walk?" I asked, as I dumped the spices from the pan into the grinder.

"He could go on fifty walks a day and it wouldn't be enough for him." Conner sat down on a stool. "Can I help?"

"I got it," I said.

He chuckled.

"What?" I narrowed my eyes at him.

"Control freak," he said, but in a teasing tone I hadn't heard in at least a year.

I took a breath. "Fine, while I grind everything up, boil four cups of water."

He saluted me and came around the counter. We worked quietly, and I stopped worrying about awkwardness and focused on my cocoa. It was my favorite hot chocolate drink, even though Audrey complained it was too much work and too much waiting. She thought it was easier to pour hot water over disgusting powder mix.

Conner took out a strainer and an extra bowl. He and I had made this recipe together two years ago, with Audrey watching. I couldn't believe he remembered the steps. I poured the cooked hot chocolate mixture through the strainer and into the bowl. Then I ladled out equal portions into two mugs and slid one over to Conner.

Before he sipped, he glanced at me. "We're okay, right?"

I nodded and then closed my eyes to drink my hot chocolate. Chocolaty, spicy, and not overly sweet. A perfect blend of flavors.

I peeked over my mug and watched as Conner sipped. Not everyone liked the taste. It was not your usual hot chocolate.

"Just as good as I remembered." He nodded at his mug. "I've missed this."

I wasn't sure if he meant the hot chocolate or us. And as I followed Conner to the kitchen table, I realized the answer was really important.

"Why are you mad at Audrey?" I asked.

He shook his head. "Forget I mentioned it."

"But maybe I can help you and Audrey make up."

He snorted. "Typical Cake."

"What's that supposed to mean?"

"It's what you do. Rush in to the rescue and try to fix everything."

I scowled. "You make it sound like a bad thing."

Conner turned his mug in his hands.

"What are *you* doing home?" Audrey's voice sliced into the kitchen.

Conner, his back to his sister, closed his eyes. His chest rose and fell as he took a deep breath. Audrey's hair was brushed and her face washed. She looked fresh and neat, while I felt rumpled and frumpy in my PJs.

"You want some hot chocolate?" I asked.

"Not if it's your weird homemade kind." She flounced to the fridge. At least she was talking to me.

Lumpy heard the fridge open and trotted over. Audrey, holding an OJ carton and an apple, stumbled as she ran into Lumpy. She dropped the carton and splattered juice all over the floor.

"Get out of the way, you stupid dog," Audrey snapped.

Conner strode across the kitchen, and Lumpy bounded over to him, tail wagging, oblivious to Audrey's glare.

"Don't call him names," Conner said.

"You should talk," Audrey said. "You're the king of name-calling."

"And you're the queen of self-obsession!" Conner led Lumpy out of the kitchen.

"Drop dead, Conner, and take your stupid dog with you!" Audrey screamed as the front door slammed. The house shuddered and Audrey stormed back to her room. How their parents could sleep through this was beyond me. Maybe they were just used to it.

I grabbed the OJ carton from the floor and cleaned up. I washed and dried my dishes and our mugs, then wiped down the counter. I wished things weren't so weird. I wished Audrey wasn't upset. I couldn't think of how to smooth things over with her, but I knew I should try.

Instead of going to talk to Audrey, I made my way into the den. The built-in bookshelves showcased photos of family vacations and special occasions. Because Mr. and Mrs. Lassiter ran a photo business, printing and framing photos and teaching digital photography, their house was filled with printed pictures.

Each family member had their own shelf to put photos on. All the pictures on Audrey's shelf were of her and me and Jenna. Our sixth-grade school portraits. The three of us in matching Halloween costumes the year we dressed as pieces of sushi. Jenna's mom used to make our costumes before the divorce. There was a photo of us horseback riding in San Diego, and another of us on the beach. Audrey wore a bikini, Jenna, a sporty black tankini, and I had on an oversize T-shirt over my striped one-piece.

Conner's shelf hadn't changed much over the years. Toward the back was his T-ball team photo from ages ago. It was how he'd met Teddy and Doug. In front was a more recent photo of the three of them at the park on the basketball court, looking sweaty but happy. The rest of the pictures were of Lumpy. Lumpy as the skinny puppy Conner had found, wrapped in a dirty blanket by a trash bin. Lumpy looking gangly months later, tennis ball in his mouth. His ears were perked, like he was listening to something Conner said.

The front door squeaked open.

"Hey."

I swung around with a grin. "You came back."

Jenna's hair was now a deep, dark violet.

"I guess I know what you did last night," I said. "It looks good."

Jenna tugged on her hair. "Thanks. I had to do something. I couldn't sleep." She glanced behind her. "How is she?"

"She was okay until she and Conner had a screaming match this morning."

"Let's get this over with."

"Really?"

"I thought about this all night, Keiko. I feel bad for Audrey, I really do, but I haven't done anything wrong. Except maybe not telling her about how I felt about Elliot right away, but I didn't get the chance. Plus I wasn't really sure how I felt. I'm not like you guys. I need to think about things."

I followed Jenna down the hall, a mixture of dread

and hope filling me. *Please make everything be okay.* Our footsteps sounded weirdly loud on the carpet.

"She'll get over it," Jenna said. "She'll find some other guy to fall in love with. She always does."

Jenna knocked on the door and without waiting, pushed it open. Audrey was curled up on her bed. The homemade banner was shredded to pieces, and the fake flowers strewn around the room. Jenna kicked aside some crumpled tissues and sat on the floor next to the bed. I chose to sit at Audrey's desk, across the room, by the door.

"I should have told you about Elliot," Jenna began. "But I wasn't sure there was anything to tell. I only realized I really liked him after I came home."

Audrey sat up. "You should have at least told us you two were texting. That's a pretty big thing!"

"I'm sorry, okay?" Jenna mumbled.

Audrey shredded a tissue.

"And don't be mad at Keiko."

I squirmed in my seat while Audrey remained fascinated by her used tissue.

Jenna blew out a breath. I held mine.

"Are you and Elliot together?" Audrey asked.

Jenna shrugged.

"What does that mean?"

"He asked me out," Jenna said softly. "We're going to lunch tomorrow."

"Don't go," Audrey said.

"What?" Jenna and I said at the same time.

Audrey tossed her tissue on the floor. "I said, don't go out with him. Let's forget about getting dates for the dance. Forget about boyfriends." Audrey shot me a glare. "It was a stupid idea."

"None of that has anything to do with me liking Elliot. I'm not trying to achieve a goal here," Jenna said. "I like him. He likes me."

"You're choosing a guy over your friends," Audrey said.

"I'm not."

"Then don't go out with him!"

"Audrey," I started.

She leapt off the bed like she had springs. "Don't, Keiko! Stay out of this! You've done enough damage!"

"I'm just trying to help," I said, my voice shaking.

"Then be on my side!"

"I'm not on anyone's side," I said.

Audrey turned back to Jenna. "If our friendship means anything, you won't go out with Elliot."

Jenna stood up. "Forget it, Audrey. You can't force me to make a choice. It shouldn't have to be a choice."

"Shouldn't it?"

Jenna clenched her hands. "It's not like if I don't go out with Elliot, he'll go out with you."

"You don't know that," Audrey said. "You didn't give me a chance!"

"Audrey," I said. "Elliot and Jenna already knew each other. They're friends. He asked her out. Why can't you just be happy for her?"

Audrey whirled on me, her eyes blazing. "You're just like my parents! You always take everyone else's side over mine!"

"That's not true!"

"Get out of my house! Both of you!"

"Audrey," I pleaded.

Jenna mouthed "sorry" to me and left. I had to try to make this right.

"You always liked Jenna better," Audrey said.

"No, I don't," I said. "I love you both the same."

"Liar!" Audrey shouted.

I stumbled out of the room and into the hall. I didn't know what to do, but I couldn't stay. Not when she was this angry.

I went to Conner's room to grab my stuff. I rolled my sleeping bag shakily, wondering how things had gotten so messed up. Worse, I didn't know how I was going to fix it. I didn't want to imagine what it would be like if Jenna and Audrey and I weren't talking to each other. My throat felt tight and my stomach roiled.

Just then, I heard the front door slam and voices coming from the living room. It was Conner, Teddy, and Doug, and I did not want to face them. I closed Conner's door and locked it. I curled up on the floor, hoping Conner and his friends would stay in the den.

I closed my eyes and tried to calm myself. *Ignore the boys and figure out how to smooth over things with Audrey and Jenna*, I told myself. I needed a clear head so I could come up with a plan.

eleven

"Hello in there!" Conner's voice was muffled.

I pried my eyes open and realized I'd fallen asleep on the floor of Conner's room. Two knocks on the door spurred me into sitting up. Three knocks later, I stumbled to the door and unlocked it.

Lumpy pushed into the room first, followed by Conner, Teddy, and Doug. The guys wore sweat-stained T-shirts and shorts. I was still in my PJs. I wasn't wearing a bra—not that I needed one anyway—but I felt very naked. I crossed my arms and wondered how bad my bed head was.

"Nice hair," Doug said with a snicker.

I braced myself for more insults, squeezing myself tight.

But Teddy just grabbed the old sponge ball from the floor and shot it at the basket over the door. Doug jumped up and snagged the ball in midair.

"Intercepted by Nolan, and the crowd goes wild!" Doug made cheering sounds like a stadium crowd full of sports fans.

"Lassiter charges in to save the game," Conner said as he rushed Doug.

Teddy crashed into the two of them, knocking them to the floor. "But the mascot's been gaming all night and stumbles onto the court."

"You jerk," Doug said, laughing from the bottom of the pile.

I grinned. Guys were goofy.

They got up from the floor, and Conner glanced at me. Was that concern on his face? No. He probably just had to fart. I grimaced.

Teddy nodded at me. "The stench of Lassiter's room getting to you?"

That earned him a punch on the arm from Conner.

"It's your stink that's choking us, Chen," Doug said to Teddy.

It was weird sitting in Conner's room with the guys insulting each other instead of me.

"We were at the park," Conner said to me. "Hey, you should come to our game on Tuesday."

"Our own cheering section," Doug said. "Yeah, we totally deserve that."

"What game?" I asked.

"We play three-on-three with some other guys every Tuesday," Conner said, shoving Teddy into Doug for no apparent reason.

I didn't think they were serious about the invite and I was sure I wasn't going to go, but I shrugged and said, "Maybe."

"Glad to see you have new friends to hang out with already!" Audrey stood in the doorway, her face red. "At least I know you were never my real friend!"

She stomped back to her room and slammed the door. With all the door slamming that went on around here, I was surprised the house still stood.

Teddy and Doug mumbled that they were going to scrounge for food and left for the kitchen.

"I should go talk to Audrey," I said.

Conner shrugged. "It's your funeral."

I took a deep breath. "I can be friends with both of you."

"Doubt that, but good luck anyway."

"I can," I said again.

Lumpy followed me down the hall, but when he saw where I was headed, he quickly returned to Conner's room. Smart dog.

Audrey sat on her floor amid the crumpled pieces of her ruined banner. I sat down next to her.

"God!" Audrey shredded the banner into smaller pieces.

My stomach fluttered.

"You and Conner?" she said, flinging paper, if not at me, then near me. "That's just wrong."

"Me and Conner? What are you talking about? We were just talking."

She shot me a look. "In his room!"

"With Teddy and Doug!" I wrapped my arms around my stomach. "We were talking, Audrey. That's all. Don't be gross."

"It would be gross!"

"Right. We agree on that."

Audrey gathered up the crumpled paper.

"I'm sorry about not telling you about Jenna liking Elliot, but it wasn't my secret to share. She was nervous."

"She shouldn't have been!"

I clamped my lips tight to keep from saying something that would make things worse.

Audrey threw wads of paper at her trash can, missing every shot. "She should have said something to us the minute she started texting him!"

"She has a hard time talking about stuff, especially since her parents' divorce. You know Jenna."

"No. *You* know Jenna. You two have always been closer. You two talk about things and keep me out of it."

"When?" I gritted my teeth. "When have we ever done that?"

"The year of Jenna's parents' divorce! She went to your house all the time and you never invited me!"

We'd gone through this many times already. "My mom invited Jenna over. Not that I wasn't happy to have her there. And as soon as you told me you felt left out, I invited you over, too!"

"It was like sitting around a morgue."

"She wasn't celebrating," I snapped. I took a breath. "Audrey, that was then, when she was having trouble. We don't leave you out."

"Who needs her anyway?" Audrey sniffed. "She picked Elliot over us."

"No, she didn't. You made her choose. It's not fair to ask your friends to choose. Jenna should be able to have all of us."

"People choose all the time. Look at my parents," Audrey said.

"What are you talking about?"

"They always give Conner whatever he wants. Joining T-ball, going away with his stupid friends, that dog. Especially the dog! I didn't want a dog, but they didn't listen to me." Audrey paced. "And when I want something? Forget it!"

"Like what?"

"My own laptop! And stupid Conner said he was fine with sharing the desktop. Like he cared about saving them money or something. So of course my parents sided with him. No laptop for me."

I kept my mouth shut. I wasn't stupid.

Audrey stopped pacing and whipped around to me. "Well, we know who our real friends are and it's not Jenna! We're still going to Fall Ball," she said. "You and me. You'll go with Gregor, and I'll find someone else."

"Audrey, let's drop this whole thing." I didn't need a boyfriend to be happy. What I needed were my two best friends.

"We can still go to the dance."

"Why bother?"

"Do you like Gregor?"

My face got warm as I nodded.

Audrey smiled for the first time since yesterday. "You two would make a cute couple!"

"You think?"

"Don't give up. Don't let Jenna ruin it for us."

I knew better than to defend Jenna. I helped Audrey clean the rest of the litter on the floor, wishing it were just as easy to wipe away the mess we were making of our friendship with Jenna.

twelve

On Monday at lunch, I stood at the entrance of the cafeteria waiting for Jenna. Clusters of kids pushed past me. If she didn't hurry, we wouldn't have time to eat. I glanced at the clock on the wall. She was never late. Was she really going to bail on us? On me? She seemed fine in social studies, but we hadn't talked about the fiasco weekend.

I sighed and reluctantly accepted Jenna was a no-show.

"There you are!" Gregor walked up to me. "What a crowd! I couldn't find you."

My annoyance with Jenna burst into joy. Gregor was even cuter than I remembered.

"I'm starved," he said. "What's good to eat?"

I dragged my eyes away from his mouth. Must. Speak. I couldn't believe he was here. I mean, he'd said he'd meet me, but I'd kind of thought he was just being polite.

I cleared my throat. "There are four main food lines." I raised my voice above the low roar of the lunch crowd. "American food to the left. Burgers, corn dogs, fries."

"Check."

"Salad bar in the center. Specialty foods on the right. It changes every day. Looks like Asian food today. Probably soggy egg rolls and questionable sushi."

"Got it. Avoid Asian food." He nodded at me. "I suppose you qualify as an expert."

I shot him a look, but his smile dazzled me.

"What's over there?" Gregor pointed to the back section with the longest line.

"Sandwiches. Probably the best thing here. But it's so popular you'll spend most of the lunch period in line."

"That leaves us with?"

I liked the way he said "us." "Junk food," I said as I led the way.

We bought burgers and fries, and as we walked across campus to meet Audrey, a few girls we passed stared at Gregor. I lifted my head, full of joy. He was walking with me! He was eating lunch with me!

Audrey waved as we approached. Gregor sat next to me, and I couldn't stop smiling. I glanced at him as he opened a packet of ketchup. His hands looked strong. What would it feel like to hold his hand? I shifted my gaze back to my tray before he caught me staring.

We ate in silence. I racked my brain for something to talk about. I was so distracted by his cuteness that I couldn't think straight.

"So," Gregor said, "is the Fall Ball a big deal around here?"

Audrey stifled a giggle as I nudged her.

"What?" he asked. "Did I say something funny?"

"No," I said.

"It's just that we're excited about it," Audrey said. "Only the seventh and eighth graders get to go."

"Cool," Gregor said. "Do people go as couples? Or in groups?"

"Both," Audrey said. "But going as couples is always nice."

I wanted to kick Audrey. She was being too obvious.

"I'm sure you girls will have no trouble finding dates."

Audrey and I exchanged smiles.

"You'll have to beat them off with a stick," Gregor said, his voice teasing.

"Yeah, right." Audrey grabbed a french fry off my tray and tossed it at him.

He ducked and laughed. "Hey, don't waste food," he said. He took a fry and threw it at Audrey.

She leaned back just in time, and we all laughed.

Audrey smiled at Gregor. "Do you have a girlfriend?"

I dropped my burger onto my tray. No playing it cool for Audrey. Of course, I couldn't play it cool either as I turned to Gregor for his answer, hoping against hope he didn't.

He smiled. "Not at the moment."

YES! I smiled back at him.

"Here they come," Audrey said.

Conner, Teddy, and Doug passed us. Conner nodded at me, but they didn't say a word.

Gregor pulled out his phone, tapped on it, and shoved it back into his pocket. "I have to jet, but I'll see you in class, Keiko."

He said my name right! I nodded and watched him walk away.

As soon as he was out of sight, Audrey grabbed my arm. "Oh my God, Keiko. He's adorable. You're so lucky!"

I felt my smile from the top of my head down to my feet.

"Ask him to the dance in class!"

The grin slipped off my face in an instant. "Today? No way," I said.

"Why not?"

"It's too soon. Tickets aren't even on sale yet. We're not even sure he likes me like that. Besides, it would be more romantic if he asked me."

"Oh!" Audrey nudged me. "I'll bet he'll come up with a supersweet way of asking you!"

"Yeah," I said. "Maybe he'll show up at my house with flowers and a box of chocolate."

"Pshhh." Audrey waved her hand. "That's so boring. He'd better do something bigger and better than that!"

The bell rang and as we cleaned up our trash, Audrey said, "You need to flirt with him, Keiko. You're too quiet. He's not going to realize you like him."

"I don't know how to flirt." The entire idea of it made me squirm.

"You'd better step up," Audrey said. "He's hot. He's new. He's not going to stay single for long."

Her words rang in my ears as I walked into math. Nicole and Kimmie stood next to Gregor's desk. They were laughing and touching his arm. He didn't even notice me when I sat down in front of him. It was as if our lunch had never happened.

Nicole and Kimmie were pretty. They looked like they were sixteen, and I looked like I was ten. All the flirting in the world wasn't going to make Gregor notice me over Kimmie and Nicole. If only this were a John Hughes movie. He'd realize they were shallow. He'd try to get my attention, flashing that smile at me, and we'd become the perfect couple.

But real life is never like the movies.

Jenna didn't show up at the library that afternoon. Neither Audrey nor I mentioned it while we did our homework. I hoped Audrey would cool off soon. I missed our threesome. I hadn't even had a chance to ask Jenna about her date with Elliot. Not that I could have asked her in front of Audrey anyway.

I wanted to talk to Mom about all this and about Macy acting secretive, but Mom didn't come home for dinner that night. Again. Macy was quiet during the meal and Dad kept checking his phone. I missed Mom and how she used to pepper us with questions. Okay, so maybe I'd sometimes found it annoying, but today I'd welcome it over the weird silence at the table.

After dinner, I went to my room to do homework. But I couldn't focus. I kept drifting off, daydreaming about Gregor. In every daydream, I was prettier and curvier than Nicole and Kimmie. I sighed. Like that was ever going to happen.

I opened my web browser and typed "padded bras" into the search engine. Whoa! There were a lot of choices. I clicked on a link. The DD cups looked bigger than my head. I scrolled and stopped on a link that said, "Hacks for flat-chested girls." I clicked. Dr. Busty's Breast Cream claimed to increase breast size by a full cup. Right. Another link led me to an image of a contraption made of springs that looked like a torture device.

I stood and looked at myself in the mirror. I turned to the side and frowned at my reflection. Maybe I did need to get a bra with more padding than I already had. I stuck out my chest, trying to imagine what I'd look like with boobs.

Macy strode into my room without knocking. I stumbled quickly to my desk, slammed my laptop closed, and sat down so hard my desk chair rolled into my bed. She gave me an odd look.

"What's with Mom?" Macy asked as she sat down on my bed and blew her bangs out of her face.

"What do you mean?"

"She's never home anymore."

I'd been thinking the same thing, but looking at my little sister's worried face, I couldn't let her know I didn't like it, either.

"It's the promotion. She's working full-time, and she has that big grant proposal thing."

"But she's not always at work."

"What do you mean?"

"I heard Mom talking to Dad last night. She's been going to dinner with Mrs. Kitamura almost every night this week."

"She has?"

Macy nodded.

"Why would Mom go out with her friend instead of coming home? We've hardly seen her!"

Macy pulled her hair to her mouth and chewed.

"I'm sure she'll be home next week," I said quickly. "She's just been busy. Everything's fine." I wanted to believe that, I really did. "Don't worry, okay? And you can always talk to me if you want. Is something bothering you?" I wanted to ask again about her not telling me where she was after school but knew that would only shut her down.

"I just want Mom to be home, like before," Macy said.

"Don't worry," I said again as my little sister stood and walked to my door. "Everything is fine."

After Macy left, I stewed on what she'd told me. Why was Mom going out to dinner with Mrs. Kitamura instead of coming home? Was she avoiding us? And if she was, why? I'd told Macy not to worry, but now *I* was worried! I didn't need another thing to deal with. I had enough going on with trying to get Audrey and Jenna to make up and Gregor to ask me to the dance. But family was just as important as friends. I needed to make sure Macy was okay, and that meant figuring out what was going on with Mom. Unfortunately, I was just as clueless on how to do that as everything else!

thirteen

On Tuesday, I texted Audrey to say I wasn't going to be able to meet her before school. She responded with a thumbs-up emoji. I went straight to social studies knowing that this early, Jenna would be the only one in the classroom.

I sat down behind Jenna, her hair pulled up into a purple ponytail. She twisted around in her seat, smiling at me. "You're here early."

"I miss you!"

She sighed. "I miss you, too."

"How was lunch with Elliot?"

She tucked her chin and smiled. "It was nice. We talked for two hours at the café."

"Two hours? Wow!" I couldn't imagine talking to Gregor for that long. "What about?"

"Mostly newspaper stuff."

"Nice." Jenna looked happier than I'd seen her for at least a year.

"I won't be able to study with you after school most days," she said. "The paper meets then."

"Oh." That was terrible. "What about lunch?"

Jenna cringed.

"Please have lunch with us," I said. I needed something to stay the same. One thing, at least.

"Audrey's still mad at me."

"She won't stay mad forever. You have to at least show up!"

"She'll still want me to dump Elliot."

"Give her time," I said. "She's already looking for a new crush. I'll bet by the end of the week, she'll have forgotten all about Elliot."

"Maybe." Jenna fiddled with her pen.

"Hey," I said, shifting in my seat. "It's been kind of

131

weird not having my mom around since she got that promotion. Are you used to not having your dad around?" I coughed. "Wait, no, I didn't mean it like that."

Jenna shook her head. "Keiko, it's okay."

"I don't want to upset you."

"You're not upsetting me. And it's hard not having my dad around still, but yeah, I'm kind of getting used to it. You'll get used to your mom working more."

I didn't want to get used to it. I wanted my mom around to talk to, but it seemed selfish to say so when there was no way Jenna's dad was coming back. Mom's extra busyness was temporary. At least, I hoped so.

"I texted Audrey yesterday," Jenna said, changing the subject and relieving us of the awkwardness hanging in the air.

"That's great," I said. "What did she say?"

"She didn't answer."

"Maybe she didn't see it." But we both knew Audrey wouldn't have missed a text.

"I've already apologized," Jenna said. "It's Audrey's move."

Students starting filing into the room.

"Isn't there a middle ground?" I whispered as Mr. Jay walked in.

"You should be asking Audrey that."

But I didn't get a chance to talk to Audrey about it during second period. And as much as I wanted to fix Audrey and Jenna's fight, there was no way I'd bring it up during lunch if Gregor was there. The last thing I wanted was for him to find out personal stuff that made us look bad. I really hoped he would have lunch with us.

When I got to the cafeteria, for some reason, the sandwich line was short. I breezed through, getting a turkey on rye. As I cashed out, Gregor was waiting for me. My heart flipped and I nearly dropped my tray.

"Hey," he said, peering at my lunch. "You got a sandwich. That looks good!"

"I'll share it with you." I squeed to myself, trying not to let my elation show. I wanted to be cool and act like I shared my lunch with cute guys all the time. Maybe things were working out for me after all! Take *that*, Nicole and Kimmie!

When we sat down with Audrey, I placed half my sandwich on Gregor's tray and grinned.

"So, how do you like PV Middle so far?" Audrey asked.

Gregor took a handful of his fries and placed them on my tray. Fortunately, he was looking at Audrey as she asked him her question, otherwise he might have seen my face flush with pleasure. I picked up a french fry, thinking how his hand had touched it and now I was putting it to my lips. Like a kiss. I had never loved a strip of potato like this before. I ate it slowly, savoring.

"It's way larger than my old school," Gregor said. "And California is definitely different from Michigan, but it's cool here. The people are pretty great."

That made me smile even more. He thought we were great! But then I stopped midchew. Was he talking about me and Audrey, or was he talking about a lot of people, like maybe Nicole and Kimmie? How many people did he know?

.While I obsessed about who else he might be hanging out with, Audrey chatted about classes and schedules. I ate my half sandwich without adding a word. As we ate, I felt the dampness from the grass seep through the seat of my light blue pants, the ones Audrey had helped me pick out when we'd gone shopping. I'd paired them with my gray-and-white, polka-dot slip-on Vans.

Gregor looked at his phone. "I have to go." He turned

to me as he stood. "Thanks for sharing your sandwich, Keiko. You're sweet."

I grinned up at him. I didn't want him to see me blush, so I stood and busied myself with my tray. Audrey gasped.

Gregor and I both looked down at her. Her eyes were wide. She flicked her gaze to my pants.

"What?" I asked, craning my neck. "Did I sit in something gross?" It figured. New pants and all.

Audrey leapt to her feet and whispered in my ear, "Your period started."

My face went up in flames. Too bad not literally, because that would have helped me disappear from Gregor's questioning gaze. I sat down quickly.

"What's wrong?" Gregor asked.

"Nothing!" I said. "Everything's fine! See you later!"

Audrey dug through her backpack, but if she whipped out a pad or tampon right now I was going to kill her. "I don't have my sweater," she said. "I left it in my locker."

Oh my God. I was going to die. Why was Gregor still standing here?

"I have a jacket," Gregor said, unzipping his windbreaker.

"NO!" I shouted. "It's okay!" I was not going to wrap Gregor Whitman's jacket around my waist. I mean, I would have loved to any other time, but not for this. If he would just leave, I could think and figure out what to do.

Gregor pulled off his jacket and tossed it to me. "I have two older sisters," he said. He flashed me a sympathetic smile and walked away.

I stared after him, long after he disappeared in the crowd, and ran my fingers against the silky smoothness of his jacket.

Audrey sighed loudly. "That was so romantic!"

Her words snapped me out of my daze. I was torn between hugging Gregor's jacket and wanting to disappear forever from embarrassment. How could I face him again?

"What are you going to do?" Audrey asked. "The bell's about to ring. Do you have anything with you?"

Right. Disappear from embarrassment it was. "Yeah." I carried supplies in my backpack for this very reason. "I have sweatpants in my gym locker. If I hurry I can make it to class in time."

"Sweatpants?" Audrey wrinkled her nose.

"This is not the time to harp on my fashion sense."

I wrapped Gregor's jacket around my waist. "See you at the library after school?"

Audrey shook her head. "I have a Fall Ball committee meeting. You should see what Gregor does after school."

Any other time, maybe, but I was not going to face Gregor on purpose anytime soon. Unfortunately, I'd have to see him in math.

When I got there, in my sweatpants, I took a deep breath before stepping into the classroom. Gregor said he had older sisters. He gave me his jacket. And Audrey called his gesture romantic. Maybe everything wasn't ruined and I still had a chance. I hugged his jacket.

But, just like yesterday, Gregor didn't acknowledge me when I got to class. Nicole and Kimmie were there first, monopolizing Gregor. Nicole was in my seat. I stood there hoping she'd notice and move, but no such luck. Even Gregor didn't take his eyes off Nicole long enough to see me standing there.

"I totally love your shirt," Nicole said.

Gregor flashed his perfect teeth at her. "It's just Gap."

"You make it look good," Kimmie said.

Wow. I couldn't imagine saying any of those things to Gregor. Just listening to Nicole and Kimmie made me squirm.

The bell rang and Nicole sprang out of my seat, bumping me. "Sorry," she said. "Didn't see you there."

I slid into my seat and handed Gregor his jacket. "Thanks," I said, feeling invisible and ugly next to Nicole and Kimmie.

Gregor smiled at me, right at me, and said, "My pleasure."

As I turned back around in my seat, Nicole and Kimmie gave me dirty looks. A smile bloomed on my face. Despite the humiliation of my period starting during lunch with Gregor, I ticked off all the good stuff: Gregor finding me in the cafeteria, walking with him, sharing a sandwich with him, and as Audrey pointed out, the romantic gesture of him giving me his jacket. Ending with a smile directed at me, in front of Nicole and Kimmie.

It might have been the most embarrassing day I'd ever had, but it was also the best day ever!

fourteen

When school ended, I was still smiling. I'd scored six points during a basketball scrimmage in PE, and Coach Yang told me that if I kept that up, maybe I could try out for the team. That wasn't going to happen, but it was rare for me to get singled out like that in a good way.

I was still smiling when I got to my hall locker.

"Hey," Conner said.

What was he doing here? He sidestepped out of my way. I spun my combination and opened my locker.

"Where were you at lunch?" Conner asked. "We swung by to say hi like usual, but you weren't there."

I blinked at him. Swooping by at the end of lunch and throwing insults was saying hi? I swallowed my retort to keep the peace. I liked it better this way.

"I had to do something," I said.

"You ready?"

"For?"

"You're coming to our game at the park, right?"

I'd forgotten about that. It seemed like a lifetime ago that I'd talked to Conner at Audrey's.

"We can walk over together if you want," he said.

Audrey had her committee meeting and Jenna was busy with the newspaper. It wasn't like I had any plans, so I nodded.

We walked into the warm fall air and neither of us said a word for the next block, the sounds of school growing fainter with each step. I glanced at Conner. He stood tall, not at all slouchy. Why did I always picture him slumped? Not that I pictured him often. Conner turned to catch my eye, and I swiveled my head away.

"You're quiet," Conner said.

"So are you."

"True."

We arrived at the park the back way and cut across the asphalt parking lot toward the basketball courts.

"Why?" I asked, the word popping out of my mouth.

Conner stopped at a silver convertible. "Why what?"

"Why are we quiet? Why aren't you insulting me? Not that I want you to."

"I thought we were okay?" Conner's eyes were almost golden in the sunlight.

"I guess," I said. "You're not mad at me anymore?"

"You said you could be friends with both me and Audrey."

"I can."

"Okay, then."

We stood in the parking lot, listening to kids laughing on the playground. It wasn't an uncomfortable silence. It felt, I don't know, familiar, maybe.

"So now we have nothing to say to each other?" Conner said, laughing.

"Silence is better than insults."

When we reached the outdoor courts, Teddy and Doug did that chin-jerk thing guys do. I sat down on the metal bleachers, glad for my fleecy sweatpants.

I expected to be bored, but I watched the game intently as Conner, Teddy, and Doug maneuvered all over the court, making shot after shot. I found myself noticing Conner like I never had before. His muscled legs flashed by in a blur as he made a perfect layup. He flexed his arms and bent his knees as he shot a free throw. It whooshed in the basket. Conner laughed as he high-fived Teddy after a great assist.

I shook my head. This was a nice distraction, and I was glad Conner and I were friends again. Maybe one day soon, Gregor and I would be sitting on this bench together, holding hands, watching Conner play a game. I scrunched my face. That seemed weird. I should have stayed at school today and found out where Gregor hung out. Maybe I'd do that tomorrow with Audrey's help.

By the end of the game, I'd been so lost in my head daydreaming about dates with Gregor that I had no idea who won. All six guys chatted and laughed together on the court. I stood. I'd promised to come and I had.

But now it was time to get back to real life.

"Mom?" I called as I shed my backpack in the kitchen. "Mom? Are you home?"

I really needed to talk to her about what was going on. Macy and I used to give her the details of our days right after school. It'd been so long since I'd talked to Mom that I could've become a world champion chocolatier and she'd never have known.

I climbed the stairs and peeked in my parents' bedroom. The bed was made but rumpled, which meant Dad had made it. Mom had gone to work before Dad again.

I pulled my phone out and texted her as I walked to my room.

Are you busy?

I sat at my desk and stared at my phone. No answer. I called the museum's landline and asked for her.

"Keiko?" Mom sounded out of breath. "What's going on? Is this an emergency?"

"No. But I wanted to talk to you," I said.

"Can this wait?" Mom asked. "I'm in the middle of a meeting. I'll talk to you tonight."

"Macy came home late from school and wouldn't tell me why," I said quickly. It wasn't quite the way I wanted to tell her. It sounded like snitching more than sharing a concern.

It didn't matter though. Mom had hung up. I glared at the phone. This was totally not right! I missed Mom, but it sure didn't seem like she missed us.

And I wasn't the only one who felt that way. At dinner that night, Macy brought it up with Dad.

"Where's Mom?" she asked out of the blue.

My forkful of chicken stir-fry froze halfway to my mouth.

"At a meeting," Dad said.

"Another one?" Macy asked. "How many meetings can one person have?"

"I'm sure she's working hard," I said with my mouth full.

Macy shot me a look.

Dad said, "She's off in two weekends, at least."

"Really?" I smiled. "Maybe we can all do something together. See a movie?"

"Actually," Dad said, "she's been so stressed out and tired, she's going to the spa with Mrs. Kitamura."

Macy stood up.

"Where are you going?" Dad asked.

"I'm not hungry." Macy took her plate, dumped it into the sink, and headed to her room.

It wasn't like Macy to be so snarky and short. At least not with our parents. Something was definitely up with her. Macy used to always share everything with Mom. If Mom wasn't going to be around for Macy, then I needed to step up. I would find out what was going on with her and maybe help fix whatever she was going through. Maybe she was having a rough time at school. I'd always had Audrey and Jenna, and that helped a lot. I thought about how our friendship was suffering right now. Maybe Macy and Claire were fighting?

I left Dad in front of the TV and swung by my room for a piece of TCHO extra-dark chocolate for fortification. When I knocked on Macy's door, she didn't answer. I tried the door, but she'd locked it.

"Mace? Are you there? I want to talk to you." I pressed my ear against the door. Why wasn't she answering me?

I stalked back to my room, ate another square of chocolate, and returned with a paper clip. When we were younger, I used to hide in Macy's closet and scare her. She'd gotten a lock on her door and I'd learned to pick it so I could sneak in and scare her still. It became a game for us. She'd set booby traps for me. The best one was when she'd balanced a small plastic bucket of gumdrops over the closet door so that when I opened it all the way, it fell on me. We'd laughed until our stomachs ached.

I couldn't remember why we stopped. It was after Grandpa Carter had moved in with us after Grandma died. He'd always been a little grumpy, but then he started drinking a lot. Fun and games had pretty much stopped around then.

I picked the lock easily and nudged the door open with my toe. Not that I really expected a booby trap. I poked my head into her room. She wasn't there. She wasn't in the closet either, although I'd half hoped she'd jump out at me, laughing at my terrified face.

Why'd she lock the door? I ran over to the window. It was open, and the screen was popped out. She climbed out the window? My heart hammered. Why? I needed to find out what she was up to before she got into trouble, or hurt. I grabbed my phone from my room and called Audrey. We always had each other's backs.

"Did you hang out with my brother after school?" Audrey said without greeting me.

"Kind of."

"Why?" she said. "Why are you being such a terrible friend?"

"I didn't do it to hurt you."

"Didn't you? You know I hate him!"

"This isn't why I called you," I said.

"So what? Why don't you call Conner instead?" Audrey clicked off.

I stared at my phone. She'd never hung up on me before. Everything was getting so messed up! Forget it. I could do this on my own. No need to bother Dad—I didn't want him to worry.

It was up to me to save Macy from whatever trouble she was getting into.

fifteen

When I got to Claire's, Mrs. Margolis didn't seem at all concerned that Claire and Macy weren't there.

"Do you know where I can find them?" I asked.

"At school, of course," Mrs. Margolis said.

Okay, then. I walked the familiar path to Sandpiper Elementary two blocks away. When I got there, it was pretty easy to pick a place to start. Lights shone from the auditorium. Inside, a small group of kids gathered near the front. Onstage, others played out a scene.

My sister stepped out onto the stage and I dropped into a seat near the rear of the auditorium. There was no set, no costumes. Macy and the two other students onstage held scripts, and Macy spoke in a voice I would never have recognized, sure and strong. As she recited her lines, my sister faded away, and in her place appeared a girl embarking on a quest.

"Excellent, Macy," the teacher said when the scene was done. "Much improved. We'll take it from there tomorrow. I want everyone to be off book by the end of next week."

I felt numb as the cast scattered. When the lights brightened, I stood and caught Macy's attention. Her eyes widened in surprise as she slid off the stage and started walking up the aisle toward me, dragging her feet.

I walked in a daze. When I met Macy halfway, she started to pull her hair into her mouth.

"You were great," I said before she could get saliva all over her hair.

She dropped her hair. "Really?"

"Fantastic! Seriously."

"Thanks," she said, her face filling with relief. "I thought you were going to yell at me."

"Well, maybe for sneaking out of the house. Especially for climbing out your window. That's dangerous!" I said sternly. Then I asked more gently, "Why sneak out for this?"

"You didn't approve of me joining the drama club. I didn't want you to stop me."

"What? I never said I didn't approve."

"Yeah, when I first mentioned it."

I shook my head. "I was just worried you'd get your feelings hurt if you didn't make the cut."

"Right. That's why I didn't want to say anything to you," Macy said. "You worry and you want to protect me. That's what you do."

"That's not true," I said.

"You used to do that when Grandpa lived with us. As soon as he started drinking, you'd distract me. We'd play games in your room or go out into the backyard."

"You knew what I was doing?"

She quirked her lips. "Yeah."

I thought I'd been so clever back then. When Grandpa started drinking, he'd get super negative. Everything was horrible, people were evil, life was terrible. It was depressing, and I didn't want Macy to have to see Grandpa like that.

"I didn't mind," Macy said softly. "It was nice,

hanging out with you. But, I don't want you to worry about me. I don't need you to fix things for me anymore. I wanted to audition on my own without you worrying."

"I worried anyway," I said. "Do Mom and Dad at least know about this?"

Macy shrugged. "Dad knows. He signed my permission slip.

"You hid this from me." The hurt leaked out into my voice.

"Only because I didn't want you to stop me."

I needed to show her I was supportive and that I believed in her. "So, this play seems pretty cool. What is it?"

"Mr. Diggs wrote it. It's an original. Awesome, right?"

"Very."

Claire joined us. "My mom's here. Hi, Keiko! Isn't Macy good?"

I nodded. "Are you in the play, too, Claire?"

She giggled and shook her head. "No. But I'm part of the stage crew, so Macy and I can still hang out together."

"That's nice," I said.

Somehow my little sister had things figured out way better than I did.

I wished Jenna, Audrey, and I had managed to join a club together at the start of school. Then maybe we'd all be talking right now.

I watched Macy and Claire, their heads together, as they followed Mrs. Margolis out of the auditorium. Seeing them gave me renewed determination to mend the rift. Audrey would listen to me. Tomorrow, I'd get everything back on track.

sixteen

Wednesday morning, Audrey wasn't waiting for me at my locker. I checked my phone, but there were no texts from her. I dashed off a quick "Where are you?" then exchanged my books and checked my phone again. Nothing. Where was she?

"Hey! You bailed on us!" Teddy called out, as he and Conner and Doug came up to me.

"Where'd you go after our game?" Conner asked.

"Home. You guys did great." At least I hoped they did. "Um, did you win?"

They laughed. "Yeah," Conner said, grinning. "We won."

I hitched my backpack over my shoulder and peered down the walkway.

"Audrey's with that new guy, in case you're looking for her," Conner said.

"What do you mean?"

"We saw her sitting with him where you guys usually eat lunch."

"But, she meets me here," I said.

Conner shrugged.

I checked my phone again for a text, a voice mail, an email, anything. Nowhere did Audrey let me know where she was going to be this morning.

"We gotta run," Doug said suddenly. "History quiz this morning."

"AHHH!" Teddy banged his fist against a locker. "I totally forgot!"

Conner and Doug razzed Teddy as they scurried down the hall, Teddy pulling notes out of his backpack frantically.

Conner turned, letting his friends get ahead of him. "Cake?"

"What?" I checked my phone again.

"We eat lunch by the gym, on the top bleachers."

Before I could reply, Conner had caught up with Doug and Teddy.

~~

When I plopped down into my chair in social studies, I noticed Jenna had a glow about her. Audrey would have appreciated the cliché. I felt a pinch of anxiety when I thought about her, but I was sure she'd explain what was going on with her when I saw her during second period.

Jenna grinned like she had just jumped out of a plane unwillingly but loved it.

"Um, what's up with you?" I said.

She laughed and her cheeks turned pink.

"Okay, now you have to tell me!"

Jenna whispered, "He held my hand!"

"Oh, Jenna! This morning?" I smiled.

"When he walked me to class."

"That's so sweet!" Elliot was spending time with her. He was showing her he liked her. Jenna had a boyfriend. I was happy for her, I really was, but at the same time, I felt like she was leaving me behind.

"We eat lunch in the journalism room," she said. "You can eat with us."

I wanted to, but I also didn't want to abandon Audrey. "Nah. Three's a crowd and all."

We smiled sadly at each other, realizing that clichés weren't as entertaining without Audrey.

"She'll come around," I said, recalling my determination to mend this. It might be easier to sway Jenna. "Maybe you and Elliot can eat with us." But even as the words came out of my mouth, I knew it would be a bad idea.

"Another time," Jenna said. We both knew that meant a long, long time from now, whenever Audrey got over Jenna and Elliot.

Like it or not, Audrey was the one I had to convince. I'd talk to her before class.

Or not. When I got to language arts, Audrey didn't even look up at me when I sat down next to her. The vibe was so weird that I didn't poke her like I normally would if I thought she was distracted. I shifted in my chair, making it squeak, hoping that would get her attention. It didn't. I took out a pen and notebook and dropped them onto my desk. No reaction.

I flipped open my notebook, smacking it against the desktop, but this time not to purposely get her attention. *I* was the one who was annoyed with *her* for hanging up on me last night. How was it that she was giving *me* the silent treatment? I hadn't done anything wrong!

I turned to her. She had her notebook open, and she was drawing a heart around Gregor's name in bubble letters. I blinked. Nope. Not a mirage. His name in pink ink was there on the page. What was going on?

I couldn't focus on anything Ms. McQueen said during class. When the bell rang, I swallowed my pride and anger and turned to Audrey. But she was already out of her seat and heading for the door, without a word to me.

Anxiety flooded me, making me feel twitchy. Here I was thinking that I needed to fix Audrey and Jenna's fight, but now I was worried about me and Audrey. I needed to make her talk to me so I could figure out what was going on with her. If she was mad that I spent time with Conner, fine. But that didn't explain Gregor's name in her notebook. Gregor's name with little hearts. Was she trying to punish me? I didn't get it. Did she like Gregor? Or was she trying to be a good friend and telling me to make my move? I was so confused!

I couldn't let this go on any longer. I needed resolution. I needed my best friend. I skipped going to the cafeteria and ate half a bar of chocolate as I made my way to our lunch spot. I sat there, waiting. I checked my phone. Where was Gregor? Maybe he was waiting for me at the cafeteria. I didn't have his number, or I would have texted him.

As more time went by, I contemplated taking out a book to look like I was reading, but I didn't want to sit there by myself anymore. I wasn't stupid. Audrey and Gregor weren't coming.

I brushed off my jeans and started walking, acting like I had somewhere to be. I could go to the journalism room and see Jenna, but I dreaded telling her what was going on with Audrey. She was annoyed with Audrey already; I didn't want to give her more reason to be angry.

"Yo, Cake!"

Conner, Doug, and Teddy sat on the bleachers, exactly where Conner said they'd be. I told myself I hadn't purposely ended up here, but I knew I was lying to myself. Having someone to sit with, even Conner and the Maybe-Not-Actually-Morons, for the last ten minutes of lunch was better than wandering around alone.

Conner moved over to make room for me.

"Do you ever wonder what babies think the first time they see a mirror?" Doug asked. "Like, doesn't it freak them out?"

"I don't know," Teddy said. "He probably doesn't even know what he looks like."

"You know what should freak him out?" Conner asked. "The first time he sees his mom in the mirror!"

Doug laughed. "Right? I mean, there's Mom! No wait. Now there are two Moms! Mind. Blown!"

"I think babies laugh, though, when they look in a mirror," I said.

All three guys turned to me.

"That's not how you play," Conner said, still smiling.

"Oh? How do you play?" I asked.

"Well, there aren't any real rules," Teddy said. "Except no backing up anything with facts or science."

"Yeah, like this morning Lassiter wanted to know who was the first person who looked at an artichoke and said, I know, let's eat that prickly-looking weird thing," Doug said.

"Worse," Teddy said. "Who wanted to eat a lobster or a crab? Why not a stinkbug or an earwig?"

"Except crabs are bigger and have meat in them," I said.

The guys looked at me blankly.

"Oh!" I laughed. "Right. Got it. Like who decided to make cough syrup taste like fake bubble gum? Disgusting on both counts."

They laughed.

"Now you get it," Conner said.

The next ten minutes sped by. We were still laughing when the bell rang. The guys acted like having me here was normal. Were they clueless? It didn't matter. All that mattered right now was that I wasn't alone.

seventeen

When I walked into math, Gregor was sitting without his usual groupies, Nicole and Kimmie. That was a first.

"Hey," Gregor said when I sat down. "Where were you at lunch?"

"Where were *you*?"

"Audrey said you wanted to meet in the picnic area, but you never showed up."

Hold up. What? Audrey hadn't said anything to me. On purpose. What was she up to? And why?

"*I* was at our usual spot," I said, gritting my teeth.

Gregor studied me, and I squirmed. I didn't want

him to know my personal business. What was going on between Audrey and me was between the two of us.

"I guess I forgot," I said. I'd deal with Audrey later.

He smiled. "What did you get for the last problem on the homework?"

I took out my folded worksheet and handed it to him, our fingers grazing. When I glanced at him, he was looking right at me, staring deeply into my eyes. I quickly looked away and then wanted to kick myself. I should have met his eyes and smiled flirtatiously. How did a person smile flirtatiously? Was it like a regular smile? Or different? Maybe I should practice in a mirror.

"Thanks," he said, interrupting my thoughts. He handed my paper back. "Glad to know I got it right. You're good at math."

"Not really." I mean, I was decent, but it wasn't my best subject—science was.

He nodded. "It's probably in your DNA."

"What?" Was he implying that I was good at math because I was Asian?

Nicole and Kimmie walked into the room and came straight for Gregor.

"Where were you?" Nicole asked Gregor.

"Sorry, I got tied up," Gregor said, flashing a smile at them. It was like he knew that smile could get him what he wanted.

"Oh, okay," Nicole said, giggling.

"You're the highlight of our lunch period," Kimmie said. "That and walking with you to class."

So now I knew where Gregor went the last ten minutes of lunch. Except he didn't meet them today, when he was alone with Audrey. Time with Audrey was better than time with me, or even Nicole and Kimmie. I sunk down in my seat.

After school, I went to the library to find Audrey. I was a little mad at her, but mostly I wanted her to talk to me. Whatever was going on, it was fixable. It had to be. I took a deep breath to try to calm my nerves.

Of course she wasn't there. I texted her and called her. No answer. I didn't understand why she was shutting me out. And I really didn't understand what she was doing with Gregor.

When I got home, the first thing I did was check Macy's room. She wasn't there. I texted her, and she texted right back. She was at rehearsal. I sent her a thumbs-up emoji. At least I knew she was okay.

I poured a glass of milk and headed up to my room. Dad's coworker had brought back a chocolate bar from his business trip, and I was dying to try it.

I sat down at my desk and held the bar in my hand. It was hefty. Lake Champlain Maple Caramel. Saliva pooled in my mouth. I tore off the paper wrapper and peeled back gold foil to reveal dark chocolate. I broke off a square, and a glob of caramel oozed onto my finger. When I popped it into my mouth, I let it melt on my tongue. The chocolate was amazingly smooth with no bitterness, and the caramel had a touch of maple flavor. A tad sweet, but sometimes sweet was exactly what I needed.

I ate the entire bar in one sitting. Something I never did. A rush of sugar made my brain buzz with pleasure. But a minute after I swallowed the last luscious bite, the buzz faded.

I wondered if Dad could order more of this chocolate. I tapped in the name of the company in my web browser. The company was based in Vermont! And that made me think of snow. And Grandpa. Heaviness pressed on my chest. I wished I had more chocolate.

The doorbell rang and I leapt up, grateful for the distraction. Maybe Audrey had finally gotten over whatever was bugging her. I'd forgive her immediately, of course. I needed my best friend back. I ran to the door, happiness making my heart light.

I yanked open the door. Conner stood there, grinning, as Lumpy jumped on me, tail wagging so hard his hind end swayed. It was the wrong Lassiter, but nothing beat having a dog greet me like this. I hugged Lumpy and laughed as he licked my face.

Conner pulled Lumpy into a sit. "You want to come with me to take Lumpy for a walk?"

"Why?"

"Um, 'cause Lumpy likes walks?"

"No, I mean, why are you asking me?" I leaned against the doorframe.

Conner frowned. "You don't have to come."

It wasn't like I had better things to do. "Can I hold his leash?" I asked as I slipped on my Vans.

Conner handed the leash to me, and Lumpy yanked me down the porch steps.

"Tell him to heel," Conner shouted as he closed my front door.

"Heel!" Miraculously, Lumpy immediately stopped pulling and dropped to a walk at my left. "That's amazing," I said when Conner caught up. "Did you teach him that?"

"Yep." Conner looked very pleased with himself.

We walked to the park. Lumpy trotted along, mouth open like he was grinning. My heart surged.

"I wish I could have a dog," I said.

"I volunteer at the Bluff Lane Animal Shelter on Saturdays. There are always good dogs up for adoption."

"You volunteer?"

"If you get your parents to agree to let you get a dog, I could help you pick one out."

"That would be awesome." Of course, my mom would have to actually be around for me to ask her such a thing.

Lumpy picked up the pace as soon as he saw the park's gates. This side of the park was mostly empty, except for a few kids on the playground. Conner led the way to a grassy hill and unclipped Lumpy's leash.

As Lumpy galloped across the grass, Conner explained, "This is the Pacific Vista Dog Park. Lumpy's allowed off-leash as long as we stay on this side of the hill."

Lumpy waited a few yards away, staring at us, tail wagging.

"Watch this." Conner pulled a soft multicolored disc out of his back pocket and flung it. Lumpy chased it and caught it in midair.

"Can I try?" I asked.

Lumpy loped back with the disc and dropped it at Conner's feet. Conner swooped down to pick it up and handed it to me, slobber side in his hand. I tossed it, and as it wobbled its way across the park, Lumpy gave chase again and caught it.

I whooped and grinned.

We continued tossing the disc for Lumpy, showering him with praise every time he returned with the toy. It was getting very wet with his slobber. One time when I flung it, a spray of dog spittle flew off the toy, splattering both of us. We ducked and laughed.

Lumpy trotted back yet again, but his ears pricked up and he ran past us.

"Hey!" I turned to chase Lumpy but stopped when I saw him prancing around Doug and Teddy.

"Yo," Doug said. "Thought we'd find you here."

Teddy spun a basketball in his hands. "Hoops?" he asked.

Conner turned to me. "You want to?"

Did I want to throw a basketball around with these three? Was this some kind of setup? "What are you guys up to?"

"Basketball," Teddy said, giving me an odd look.

Conner clipped the leash back onto Lumpy's collar and started walking with Doug and Teddy. "Come on, Cake!"

I followed them across the park to the outdoor courts where I'd watched them play their game yesterday. Today, they were empty.

Conner told Lumpy to stay and, without tying him up, walked onto the court. I sat on the bench next to the dog.

Conner waved at me. "We won't have even teams if you don't play."

"I can't play," I said.

"We'll go easy on you," Doug said, doing a fake evil laugh and rubbing his hands together.

Coach Yang had praised me in PE, and I recalled the rush I'd felt. Pent-up energy bubbled inside me. It might feel good to play. The guys stood there, waiting. I shrugged, then walked over to join them.

"Half court," Conner said, probably for my benefit.

I stood out of bounds and tossed him the ball, but Doug flew in and snagged it. I ran to guard Teddy, but before I got to him, Doug made a basket. Teddy and Doug exchanged high fives.

I steeled myself for Conner to yell at me for screwing up, but he just grinned.

"Get ready to be shamed," Doug said, spinning the ball on his finger.

That did it! I didn't want to lose. I stuck to Teddy on defense, and Doug was forced to take a shot and missed. Conner grabbed the rebound. I ran to mid-court, wide open, and caught his pass. I wasn't ready to dribble so I threw the ball back to Conner as Teddy rushed toward me. Conner shot a three-pointer. *Swish!*

"That's the way you do it!" Conner shouted.

I grinned. By the time we called game, I was still grinning. Doug and Teddy won by a small margin. Conner had made all our points, but I'd held my own, passing and snatching rebounds. We all dropped onto the cool grass. Conner snapped his fingers, releasing

Lumpy from his stay. Lumpy crawled over and rested his head on Conner's legs.

"Not bad, Cake," Teddy said.

"Dude, what if basketball was like soccer and you couldn't touch the ball with your hands?" Doug asked.

"That *is* soccer, you moron," Conner said.

"No, like using the basketball and hoops!"

"Maybe like combine all the sports. Football, baseball, basketball, soccer," Teddy said.

"Yeah! Use a football, hit it with your head," Conner said.

"And use a bat to block!" Teddy leapt up and acted it out.

"Hockey!" Conner and Doug shouted at the same time.

Lumpy came over and nuzzled my neck with a cold nose. I stroked his smooth head as I leaned back to stare at the blue sky, still smiling, while trying to catch my breath.

I'd thought I hated these guys, but it turned out things changing didn't always have to be a bad thing.

eighteen

Audrey wasn't at my locker again the next morning. I ate half a bar of chocolate to give me strength and nearly ran to second period to have time to confront her before the bell rang. And once again when I sat down next to her, Audrey wouldn't look at me. I put my hand over the page of the book she was reading, forcing her to glance up.

"Okay, what's going on, Audrey?" I asked. "Why are you avoiding me?"

Audrey smiled. "Oh my God, Cake, I'm not avoiding you. I'm trying to help you!"

"You are?"

"Yes! Since you can't seem to show Gregor that you like him, I'm going to convince him that you're great so he'll ask you to the dance."

"Oh." I was still confused. "So why not just tell me? I mean, I totally didn't know where you were."

"I know! Sorry! I was just so focused on nudging him in the right direction. I thought you'd figure it out!" Audrey patted my hand. "Give me a few more days, and he'll be asking you to Fall Ball before you know it."

Then the bell rang. Ms. McQueen had us move our tables in a circle, and Audrey smiled at me as we pushed our desks next to each other. I was relieved she wasn't angry with me. I wasn't sure her idea would work, but I had to trust she knew what she was doing.

While I waited for Audrey's plan to come together, I fell into a new routine. I met Jenna before school in social studies, ate lunch with Conner and the boys, and walked with Jenna from PE to her locker before she met Elliot. Then after school, I went to the park and played basketball with the guys. I tackled homework in the evenings with Dad and Macy, when she didn't have rehearsals. Mom had been home only once for dinner since the start of school.

Two weeks later, on Friday, I sat down on the grass next to the basketball court, wiping the sweat off my forehead. Conner sat next to me and handed me a bottle of water.

"Okay," Doug said, panting. "Is it just me, or has Cake gotten better?"

"Definitely," Teddy said, falling down onto the grass. I grinned.

"There's a coed league here at the park," Conner started.

"Oh no," I said. "I'm not playing for real. This is just for fun."

"Fun for you maybe," Doug grumbled.

Teddy laughed.

"Playing in the league *is* fun." Conner swatted Doug.

"No," I said, twisting the cap off my water bottle. "It's all competitive and stuff. I don't like that."

"Of course you don't." Conner took a swig of water.

"What's that supposed to mean?"

"You don't like conflict. You want everything and everyone to be in perfect harmony."

I drained my bottle and wiped my mouth. "So? It's not a bad thing to want people to be happy."

"I'm starving," Doug said, flopping over on the grass like he was dying. "Make *me* happy by getting me food."

Conner nudged me. "We're going to Nolan's for dinner and a movie. You want to come?"

I glanced at Doug.

"My mom loves to feed people," he said with a shrug.

Macy was at Claire's. I loved knowing where she was. Both my parents had dinner meetings tonight (separately, of course). Dinner with the guys was better than dinner alone.

Doug lived on the opposite side of the park, so Conner and I decided to take Lumpy home and meet at Doug's. I hadn't been to Audrey's house in more than two weeks. This was the longest we'd ever gone without hanging out. Every time I texted her, she just sent a thumbs-up emoji. It all felt weird and off. How long was it going to take her to get Gregor to ask me to the dance? What if he didn't want to? As we got closer to the house, sweat trickled between my shoulder blades and chilled in the evening air. I shivered.

"You can borrow a sweatshirt," Conner said as he opened his front door. "I have to take a quick shower."

For some stupid reason, I felt my cheeks heat and I waved him on. "I'll get water for Lumpy."

I filled up Lumpy's water bowl. As he drank, I wandered down the hall to Audrey's room. I missed her.

I took my time, running my fingers along the textured wall along the hallway, my eyes on Audrey's bedroom doorway. When I reached her room, I paused and leaned in to listen for any sound that might tell me if she was in there. There was only silence. I took a breath and pushed myself forward through the open door, tightening my muscles as if ready for a battle.

The room was empty. I staggered with disappointment. But before I turned around to go back to the kitchen, something seized my attention. A picture frame on Audrey's desk. I snatched it up. Gregor. His head was thrown back and he was laughing. It had been taken in Audrey's backyard. I nearly dropped the frame. I set it clumsily back onto her desk.

I stumbled into the hall and hurried back to the kitchen. Gregor had been here. To her house. He'd let her take a picture of him. She'd taken the time to print it, frame it, and put it on her desk, where no other photos have ever sat. I barreled my way to the refrigerator, yanking the door open, searching for something even though I wasn't thirsty and we'd be leaving for Doug's for dinner. I wasn't very hungry anymore, either. I stared into the fridge like it would offer me an answer. Like it could fix whatever was ruined between me and Audrey.

"What are you doing here?"

Audrey's voice made me jump. I shut the fridge and turned to her. She stood with her arms crossed and no smile. Her voice wasn't welcoming at all, like she didn't want me here. I buried the hurt, because I couldn't stand this anymore. It felt like our friendship was falling apart.

"Audrey, what's going on?"

"What are you talking about?" Still her voice remained cold, and it froze my heart.

My eyes flicked over her shoulder, toward her room. I steadied my voice. "Is this about Jenna and Elliot?"

"Do not mention their names in my house," Audrey nearly growled.

The hurt slammed into me. "Why not? What about you and Gregor?"

"HA! So now you know what it feels like."

Audrey's triumphant tone flooded my mouth with

bitterness. "You're hanging out with him to teach me a lesson?"

She shook her head. "No. I really did try to get him to like you, but he doesn't. I mean, you showed zero interest in him. How was he supposed to know?"

"But now?"

Audrey shrugged.

"But now *you* like Gregor?" I prompted, needing to hear her say it.

Audrey took a step back just as Lumpy rounded the corner and she stumbled against him. Lumpy yelped and Audrey turned on him.

"You stupid dog!" she shouted.

Lumpy cowered. His ears went back and he lowered himself in submission, tucking his tail down.

"Move!" Audrey grabbed a place mat off the counter and waved it at the dog, hitting him on the nose. Lumpy trembled and scooted back on his belly.

I gasped and ran around the counter next to Lumpy. "Stop!" I yelled at Audrey. Lumpy leaned against me, and I wrapped an arm around him. I touched his paw, and he placed it back on the floor. He was okay. He wasn't hurt. A mixture of relief and anger flooded me.

I stood up, facing Audrey, my hands balled into fists. "What's your problem? Lumpy didn't get in your way on purpose. Don't you ever hit him! He's never done anything to hurt you!"

Audrey's mouth dropped open. I'd never yelled at her.

"Dogs are loyal. Dogs don't turn on you for stupid reasons," I continued, but at a normal volume.

"Stupid reasons?" Audrey said in a soft voice, regaining her equilibrium. "You weren't doing anything about your little crush. You hardly talked to Gregor. Someone else was going to hook him at that rate."

"Like you." I was breathing hard.

She shrugged. "If he was the least bit interested in you, he wouldn't have asked me to the dance."

"He asked you to Fall Ball?" Even as the words came out of my mouth, I couldn't believe them.

Lumpy's nails clicked across the floor, and I turned around to check on him. Conner stood in the kitchen, holding out a Lakers sweatshirt to me. "You ready?"

Audrey's glare cut through me. "Oh, it's like that? I'm obviously not important to you at all!"

She stormed off to her room, and I braced myself

as the door slammed. Conner handed me his sweatshirt.

"Don't say anything," I said as I pulled it on. It smelled like pine. I breathed in, the scent calming me a little.

We walked in silence, dry fallen leaves crunching beneath our feet. I shoved my hands into the front pockets of the sweatshirt. Images bombarded me. Gregor's laughing face. Gregor in Audrey's backyard. Gregor and Audrey. Audrey and Gregor. Eating lunch. Together. Going to Fall Ball. How could she?

"What were you guys fighting about?" Conner asked.

"Stupid stuff."

"Is it because Audrey's hanging with the new guy?"

Something in Conner's voice made me glance at him. He kept his eyes forward, but his neck muscles were taut.

"No," I said. "Not entirely." I was too humiliated to tell Conner about my crush on Gregor and how Audrey had easily lured him away. Well, maybe not lured. She was right about one thing: I hadn't done anything about my crush on him. Maybe none of this would have happened if I'd been flirty or told Gregor how I felt. Maybe this was my fault.

"So what is it, then?" Conner asked, startling me out of my thoughts.

"She's not thrilled you and I are friends."

"Told you."

Yeah, he had. Why couldn't I be friends with both of them? Not that Audrey and I were friends at this point.

Doug's house smelled like spaghetti sauce and made me hungry again. Mrs. Nolan greeted me warmly, like I was family. It made me miss my own mom and the time we used to spend together.

Doug's mom let us eat in front of the TV in the family room. Each of us had a huge square of lasagna that oozed melted cheese and tomato sauce. I cut a steaming piece with my fork, blew on it, and slid it into my mouth. Delicious!

Doug and Conner ate like they hadn't had a meal in weeks. Their plates were clean in seconds and they moved to the floor in front of the TV with the game console.

"Disgusting, isn't it?" Teddy said to me. He, like me,

was barely halfway through his lasagna. "You'll get used to it."

"Eat faster, Teddy, or you won't get a turn before the movie," Doug said.

The battle scene in the game took place on an ice-covered tundra. I stared at the animated snowscape, and my heart tugged at a memory. I ran my fingers across the tray table, feeling the coolness.

"Have you guys ever seen snow for real?" I asked.

"Yeah," all three guys answered.

"Oh."

Conner hit the pause button, ignoring Doug's complaints. "You haven't?"

"Hello," I said. "I live in Southern California." The closest I'd come was a freak hailstorm a few years ago, but that didn't count. That was not snow.

"What about Big Bear?" Conner said. "Snow Valley?"

"I've never been," I said. "What's it feel like?"

"Cold," Doug said.

"Ha-ha, funny," I said.

Doug unpaused the game and started blasting away. Conner hesitated a moment, studying me, and then returned to blowing things up on the screen.

Teddy finished eating and joined the guys in the game. I took a last bite of lasagna. I could get used to eating like this. When was the last time we'd had a family dinner? Mom was always scrambling out the door in a hurry to get somewhere else, away from us.

She belonged at home with her family. Whatever was going on, I wasn't going to let it slip through my fingers like I had with Audrey. I was going to deal with Mom.

nineteen

After watching a violent spy movie and eating raspberry cheesecake for dessert, Conner walked me home in the dark.

"Sorry about the movie choice," Conner said.

"It's okay. Car chases and explosions are fine. I'm glad you guys didn't pick a horror movie."

"Next time, you can pick the movie."

The promise of next time warmed me in a way that surprised me.

"Remember when we watched those old movies?" Conner asked.

"Yeah." I tucked my hands into the front pockets of the sweatshirt.

"You really liked *Casablanca*," he said.

"You did, too. We never did get to watch *Roman Holiday*." That was one of my mom's favorites.

"We can watch it next Friday," he said.

"Yeah, right. I'm sure Teddy and Doug would love that. It's a romance between a princess and a reporter."

"What? Guys can't like love stories?"

I glanced at Conner. Our strides matched step for step. "You guys watch rom-coms on Fridays?"

He laughed and shook his head.

"I'll pick something we'll all like," I said.

"You don't have to, you know. You're allowed to pick whatever you want when it's your turn. You don't have to make everyone happy all the time."

Look what happened when I didn't though: Jenna was off with Elliot, and Audrey wasn't speaking to Jenna and me.

"Why are you mad at Audrey?" he asked all of a sudden.

I didn't want to talk about this. "Why are *you* mad at her?"

He didn't answer.

"Conner?"

"Yeah."

"Tell me."

"You tell me first," he said. "I heard you shouting at her in the kitchen."

That was an easier conversation. "She yelled at Lumpy."

"So *you* yelled at *her*? For yelling at Lumpy?" Conner said. "But you never yell."

I shrugged, and we walked for a half block in silence.

"Your turn," I said. "Why are you mad at her?"

Conner made a noise.

"Stop stalling, Conner Lassiter."

He laughed softly. "I like the way you say my name."

My breath caught.

"Okay, fine," he said in a rush. "I'll tell you. Remember when I brought Lumpy home?"

"Yes." I'd been there when Conner walked into the house with a smelly furry bundle.

"Remember Audrey's reaction?"

"She had a tantrum," I said. "She called him a filthy

185

monster. When your parents said you could keep him, she was so mad. She thought they were playing favorites by letting you have a dog."

"That was the start of it. It just got worse. She'd kick at Lumpy whenever he got near her, and she complained about him to our parents, hoping they'd change their mind. And once when he got sick, she told me she hoped he'd die."

That didn't surprise me at all.

"It was like she wanted to make me miserable," Conner said. "I got sick of her attitude."

"And then you and I weren't friends anymore. You started calling us names."

Conner hunched his shoulders. "Yeah. That was stupid. Sorry."

A breeze stirred and kicked up dried leaves, making them skitter across the sidewalk in front of us.

"It hurt, you know," I said to Conner. "It's rude to make comments about people's appearances."

"I'm sorry, I really am." Conner reached out and touched my arm, then dropped his hand. "I never meant any of it. I mean, I don't know, I was mad. Your body is great. I mean, fine. There's nothing wrong with you," Conner babbled, his voice going squeaky. "Anyway, I'm sorry."

Fortunately, we got to my house right at that moment. My face felt like it was on fire. But as hard as it was to have brought this up, it felt good to have resolution. The only resolution I'd had in a while. The porch light shimmered, and the living room lights shone through the curtains.

"Did you talk to your parents about adopting a dog from the shelter?" Conner asked, his voice back to normal.

"Not yet."

"I'm volunteering there tomorrow. If you come by, you can see the dogs. There's this cute one you'd like."

"Really?" It would be so awesome to have a dog to love and to love me back. "What if I want to take one home?"

"I can get the shelter to put it on hold for you while you talk to your parents."

A dog of my own. I smiled. "Okay, I'll be there!"

"Come by around eleven thirty. My shift ends at noon." Conner walked backward toward the sidewalk, watching as I opened my front door. "See you tomorrow, Keiko."

It had been a very long time since Conner had called me by my real name. I stepped into the house, bathed in a warm glow.

No one was home. I sighed. I'd deal with Mom this weekend. Right now, I just wanted to feel happy and hopeful. I got ready for bed, inhaling Conner's scent as I pulled off his sweatshirt. Was that weird? Yeah. Probably. I folded it and put it on my desk to return to him later.

As I turned out the light, my phone buzzed with a text. I grabbed it, knowing it wasn't Audrey and it was too late for Jenna. Mrs. Sakai didn't allow Jenna to use any screens after 8 p.m.

It was from Conner. Just two words, good night, but they made my heart flip. I sent him back a smiley face. Talking to Conner was easy. After all the ugliness of my fight with Audrey, I couldn't wait to see him again tomorrow.

twenty

It looked like a normal Saturday morning. At least
what was normal before Mom disappeared from the
family. Mom stood at the stove, her back to me, holding
a spatula over the cast-iron griddle.

It smelled like Saturday used to. Melted butter, a
hint of cinnamon, and vanilla scenting the kitchen.

I stared at my mother's back. She wore a purple
cotton-knit skirt and a gray top. Not her usual
Saturday morning yoga pants and flowy top. In fact,
I couldn't remember the last time I'd seen her in
regular clothes, the kind she wore to relax around
the house or run errands. So while it may have looked

and smelled like a Saturday from before, her clothes said otherwise.

Mom ladled batter onto the griddle. As it hit cast iron, it sizzled.

Even though I could imagine biting into fluffy buttermilk pancakes, lightly dusted with powdered sugar and a dribbling of warm maple syrup, my mouth tightened with bitterness. Crisp anger burned at the edges of my heart. Didn't she realize she'd abandoned her family for the last month? Or maybe she just didn't care.

"Who are you and what are you doing in my kitchen?" I said, trying to sound lighthearted.

Mom turned and smiled at me. "Watch it, smarty," she said, waving the spatula. "Hey, you look nice. Where are you going?"

I sat down at the counter, smoothing the white tunic top I'd dug out of my closet. I didn't normally wear white, because it was a total stain magnet. But I kind of wanted to look nicer than the usual jeans-and-T-shirt combo Conner saw me in at school.

I countered with another question. "Are you going to be home today?"

"I have a meeting," she said, returning her attention to the stove. She flipped a pancake, and it spun onto a plate. She stuck it in the oven to keep warm. Mom poured more batter and twisted back to me. "Is everything okay?"

"Not really," I said.

Mom turned down the burner on the stove, grabbed her mug of coffee, and came over to me. "What's going on?"

I nibbled my bottom lip. I wanted to punish her for her absence and give her the silent treatment. Ignore her like she'd been ignoring us. But at the same time, I needed to talk with her. I needed her advice and support. Maybe this was the return to normal life. Maybe Mom was back and all would be fine.

"Everything's changing," I said. "Jenna has a boyfriend, and Audrey might have one, too. Audrey's not talking to me or Jenna. Macy's starring in a school play. You're never home anymore." The words flooded out of my mouth.

"Oh, Keiko. That *is* a lot to handle." She put her mug down. "I'm sure it will all settle down. Just give it time. You're going through a big transition."

That was the motherly wisdom she had to offer? I could get the same bland advice from a magazine! My life was a mess. My best friends had abandoned me, and now my mom had, too.

I scrutinized my mother. Her hair was shorter and highlighted. "You look different," I said.

Mom reached up to touch her hair. "Do you like it? I had my hair done yesterday."

"You went to get your hair done? Instead of coming home? Aren't you going to the spa next weekend?"

Mom quirked her lips. "Yes, I went to the salon. And yes, I'm going to the spa next weekend."

"But you're never home anymore," I said, trying to keep the whine out of my voice.

"I'm working, Keiko." Mom's tone turned less amused. "Getting my hair done isn't like a vacation or something."

"Well, then, where were you last night?" Or every night for that matter.

"The Purple Frog."

"That's a bar!"

Mom laughed. "I *am* old enough to get a drink after a long day."

"Mom." I frowned.

"Am I in trouble?" Mom smiled. She took a sip of her coffee.

She was joking around when I was being serious. She was never home and had zero clue or apparent interest in what was going on with her family. Did she even miss us?

I threw my hands up in frustration, knocking into Mom's mug. Coffee spilled across the counter and splattered onto my shirt. Great! Just great!

Dad strolled into the kitchen, still in his bathrobe. He surveyed the scene. "What's going on?"

I glared at the spilled coffee on the counter.

"Keiko seems to be upset with me," Mom said. "For not being home."

Dad expelled a breath.

Mom gave him a look. "Oh, are *you* mad about that, too?" Her voice was tinged with disappointment.

"You *have* been gone a lot," Dad said.

Both my parents' voices were distant. A cold dread froze my insides.

I needed to smooth things over. "Actually, I—"

"Are you serious?" Mom interrupted.

"I'm just stating the facts," Dad said. "You aren't home. The girls need you."

Mom spun around to me. "So you think I'm neglecting you and Macy?" She looked around the kitchen. "Where *is* Macy?"

"She slept at Claire's, where she's been spending a lot of time," Dad said. "Which you'd know if you were ever home."

Mom's face flushed and her eyes got bright.

I rubbed at the coffee stain on my white shirt.

"This is ridiculous!" Mom said. She stormed out of the kitchen, leaving the pancakes burning on the griddle.

Dad shook his head in annoyance and snapped off the stove with an angry flick of his wrist.

Everything was so messed up! I stalked into the living room and ran smack into Macy. Her duffel bag hung limply from her hand, her face scrunched in confusion.

"Hey, you want to go for a walk?" I asked.

Macy didn't respond but instead stared past me toward the kitchen.

"Um, how long have you been standing here?" I asked, anxiety coating my stomach.

"What have you done?" Macy threw her duffel bag onto the floor and glared at me.

"What are you talking about?"

"I heard everything! You made Mom mad! You started a fight between her and Dad!"

She pulled her hair into her mouth, talking around it. "You told me not to worry! You said everything was going to be okay!" Macy's eyes filled with tears, and she gnawed on her hair.

I didn't know what to say.

"You were supposed to fix it, Keiko," Macy said, her voice squeaking. "You're supposed to make this better, not worse!"

I had no words of comfort to offer her. Especially since Macy was right. I'd failed her. I should have protected her. I shook my head. I hated this! No matter what I did, things went wrong. My friendships were falling apart; my family was falling apart. I couldn't fix any of it!

There was no way I was going to ask for a ride to the

shelter, and I didn't want to stay. I couldn't stand facing my little sister's accurate accusations. I knew I shouldn't leave her. I should make things better. But I didn't know how!

I grabbed my shoes and jacket and ran out of the house.

twenty-one

I arrived at the animal shelter close to noon, sweaty and windblown. I'd never realized how far the shelter was. I'd started off walking briskly, anger fueling my legs, but after a few blocks, I ran out of steam. My feet felt like raw hunks of meat, and the jacket I'd needed when I first left the house was now tied around my waist.

"I wondered if you were going to show," Conner said, meeting me at the door. His eyes roved over my stained shirt and probably tangled hair. "What happened with you?"

I tried to laugh, but the sound came out more like

a sob. I slapped my hand over my mouth. I was not going to cry in front of Conner!

"You okay?" he asked, sounding like he was afraid of the answer.

"Can you still show me the dogs?" My voice trembled. I struggled to regain control. "Or do you have to leave now?"

"I can show you around. I'm done for the day."

I followed Conner around the back of the building to the dog runs. A sudden burst of barking erupted as soon as the dogs saw us coming. Dogs, tails wagging, leapt at the chain-link of their runs. Conner stopped to talk to each dog as we walked along the fence.

"This is Scamper." Conner knelt in front of a shaggy gray dog.

"Hi, Scamper." I leaned over and stuck my fingers through the chain-link. Scamper licked my fingers. I scratched the top of his head as best as I could through the fence. Petting Scamper was like a salve, and I felt the irritation in me fade.

"Unfortunately for you, but fortunately for him, he was adopted today. He's going home tomorrow."

"That's so great for him! Is this the dog you thought I'd like?"

He nodded. "Watch this." Conner stood up. "Scamper, sit."

Scamper dropped his hind end and looked expectantly at Conner.

"Lie down."

Scamper stretched out his front paws and lay on the concrete.

"Sweet!"

I wandered away from Conner, looking at the other dogs. At the very end of the row, the kennel was empty. Wait. No. There was a white ball of fluff curled in the back corner. I sat down and chirped. The ball of fluff stirred. I called to it again and it raised its head. The dog looked like a lamb. I kept chirping and it stood up and slowly walked toward me. When it finally reached the fence, the dog trembled, keeping its head low and tail tucked.

"Wow," Conner said quietly from behind me. "She never goes up to new people. Ever."

"Why not?" She sniffed my fingers through the fence, her fluffy tail wagging hesitantly. Her fur felt like silk.

"She was abandoned. Someone found her wandering the side of Beach Boulevard."

"But that's a busy street! How horrible!" My heart hammered at the thought of cars whizzing by her.

"Yeah. People are stupid sometimes. You'd be surprised at all the ridiculous reasons people give when they want to dump their pets."

"Like?"

"He got bigger than we thought he would. She barks all the time. He's too furry." Conner squatted next to me and rolled his eyes. "There are some legit reasons, too, though. Like the owner died and nobody in the family could take the dog, or an allergy or something. It's sad."

I pointed at the fluffy dog in front of me. "But this one? Nothing's wrong with her?"

Conner gave me a look. "Well, she's really nervous."

I sprang up. "I want her!"

"Really?" Conner stood slowly, surprise on his face.

"Is she available? Will they let me adopt her?"

"Are you sure, Cake? She's super shy."

"Why do you keep saying that?"

"Because you might want an easier dog. One that's

friendlier. She's been here awhile. Shy dogs are harder to adopt out."

"She's friendly with me," I said. "You said it yourself. She never goes up to new people. She came up to me. She chose me!" I felt a kinship with this dog. She was alone and no one wanted her. I knew what that felt like.

When Conner smiled at me, my head got all light. I held my breath, waiting for him to say something.

"You'll have to fill out an application, and then you and your parents have to come in for an interview before you can adopt her."

"Both my parents? At the same time?"

"Well, they like to interview the family, to make sure everyone wants the dog and will accept responsibility. They don't want a return. It's hard on the animal."

"Oh." Asking both my parents to come out this weekend seemed impossible. Who knew if they'd made up by now? And I hadn't even mentioned wanting a dog to my parents. I glanced at my dog (because I really wanted her to be mine), and our eyes met. I would not let her down.

"I'm coming back for you," I said. She wagged her tail in response.

Conner and I walked back to the front. His blue bike was the only one locked up at the rack.

"Did you walk here?" His voice rose in surprise.

I nodded, suddenly embarrassed, but I wasn't sure why.

"You're walking back home?"

I nodded again. In my haste to leave the house, I'd left my cell phone in my room. Plus I wasn't ready to call my parents.

"I'll walk with you. Hang on." Conner ran into the shelter before I could protest. When he came back out, he handed me an application. "They'll hold the dog for you until tomorrow. The shelter closes at three. Bring back the application when you and your parents come in."

"Thanks."

Conner unlocked his bike, and we started walking. I felt grungy in my coffee-stained top. I pulled on my jacket and zipped it up. A block later, neither of us had said a word.

I dreaded going back home. What if my parents were still fighting? Had Jenna's parents started off like this? Little fights that progressively got worse?

The thought of my parents splitting up made me feel sick.

"You going to Fall Ball?" Conner asked into the silence.

"No. Are you?"

"Thinking about it. Tickets go on sale in two weeks."

Conner had a girlfriend last year. "What ever happened to what's-her-face?"

He shot me a grin. "What's-her-face?"

"You know."

"Amber? We broke up a long time ago."

"Oh."

"Would you go to the dance?"

"If someone asked me?" I laughed. "That's not going to happen."

"Do you want to go?"

I shrugged. "I'm not going to cry my eyes out over not going."

"No." Conner cleared his throat. "Do you want to go to the dance? With me?"

I stopped walking. "What?"

Conner stopped walking, too, and when he faced

me, his cheeks were kind of pink. "Don't make me ask you again. You heard me."

"Is this some kind of a joke? Or a dare that Doug and Teddy made up?"

"No!" His face turned red.

"Then why would you ask me?"

"Forget it!" Conner gripped the handlebars of his bike and started walking.

I stood there for a minute. Conner had asked me to the dance. As a friend or something more? I jogged to catch up to him.

No reaction.

I peeked at his face. He was frowning.

"Conner?" My voice came out strangled.

"What?" he answered through gritted teeth without looking at me.

"I'll go with you. To the dance." My whole body flared with heat, and I wondered if my face was as red as his.

"Don't do me any favors."

I sighed loudly. "I'm not."

"This is stupid."

Oh great. Now he was taking it back.

He stopped walking again and faced me. "Let's try this again, okay?"

I nodded.

He pushed a lock of hair out of his eyes. "Will you go to the dance with me? Not because of a joke or a dare. Not because I feel sorry for you, but because I like hanging with you, okay?" He said the last part defensively.

"Okay." My face still felt like it was on fire. "I'll go with you. Because I want to."

"Fine!" Conner huffed and started walking again.

"Fine!" I walked with him, grinning the rest of the way home.

twenty-two

"Conner Lassiter asked you to the dance, and you said yes?" Jenna asked.

She sounded surprised but not disgusted.

After Conner and I split off at Magnolia Street toward our respective houses, I made a detour to Jenna's.

"Wow," she said as she sat down next to me on her unmade bed. Her mom had a lot of rules, but most of them pertained to study habits. Making the bed was not important to Mrs. Sakai.

"A huge shock," I said.

"Well, not a *huge* shock."

"What do you mean?"

Jenna leaned back against her wall, crossing her lean legs. "Conner's always liked you."

"What?" I shook my head. "No, he hasn't! He's been horrible to me."

"Not always," Jenna said. "You two were friends before he started middle school. Audrey hated that."

"That was only because—" And then I stopped, because I didn't have a good reason. Other than her being jealous. "Audrey's always had issues with feeling left out."

"She likes to be center stage. Always."

"Oh, I don't know," I said.

Jenna pulled her teddy bear onto her lap. "I saw Audrey with that new guy. Gregor, right? The guy you said you liked?"

"When? Where?"

"At lunch in the picnic grove. She was practically in his lap."

"Oh," I said.

"What's going on? You told her you liked him, and now she's throwing herself at him!"

I slid off Jenna's bed to sit on the floor. "Actually, she started out trying to help me, to get him to like me,

207

but it turns out he's interested in her. It's not really her fault."

Jenna stared at me and blinked several times.

"What?" I didn't want to talk about this anymore. "So, do you think Conner likes me? I mean, are we going to the dance as friends or what?"

"Did you ask him?" Jenna asked.

"No!"

She laughed. "Do you want it to be a date? Or do you want to go as friends?"

"As friends, I guess." I shrugged. I still liked Gregor. Didn't I? Isn't that why I was upset about Audrey?

Jenna slid down next to me.

"So," I said, "are you and Elliot going to Fall Ball? It would be fun to go together."

"We're going." Jenna grinned.

"Yay! Oh, this will be great. We can get ready together."

"And shop for dresses."

We both got quiet. Neither of us was confident about fashion. It would have been nice to have Audrey around for this.

"Any chance you and Audrey will make up anytime soon?" I asked.

"Any chance *you* will?" Jenna countered.

"She's not my favorite person right now," I said. "But I do hope we'll make up soon."

Jenna hugged her teddy bear. Her dad had won it for her at the county fair the year before the divorce. That made me think about my parents. I hoped they weren't going to split up.

I needed to deal with my parents, especially if I wanted to adopt my dog. I left Jenna's house and walked home. I dreaded facing my parents, especially my mom, but at the same time, I felt light with thoughts of Conner and going to Fall Ball.

When I walked in the door, the house was quiet. The kitchen was cleaned up, not a pan or pancake in sight. That was reassuring. My parents hadn't stormed off in the middle of breakfast. They'd taken time to clean up, perhaps even eat together.

I found Macy curled up in front of the TV, even though she hadn't turned it on. I sat down next to her on the couch. I felt bad for abandoning her earlier.

"Hey, sorry for storming off," I said. "How are you doing?"

Macy shrugged and reached up to tug her hair into

her mouth. I stopped her hand, and she smiled. "That's so you, taking care of everyone and everything."

"If that's true, I'm not doing a great job of it." I frowned. "What happened with Mom and Dad?"

"They took off after you did. Mom said she was going to work, and Dad drove off. No idea where he went." Macy tugged on her hair.

"So, wait, if they left right after I did, who cleaned up the kitchen?"

Macy smiled shyly.

"You?" I grinned. "You cleaned up?"

"I'm not completely useless," Macy said, smacking my leg. Her face grew somber. "So, are Mom and Dad, like, going to be mad at each other forever?"

"I have no idea," I admitted. "I'm sorry I got all angry at Mom for never being around, especially in front of Dad."

"Well, at least I'm not the only one who minds."

"Of course you're not." Macy probably needed someone to talk to about this as much as I did. "Sorry I haven't been here for you."

Macy shrugged again. "It's not your job."

"Sure it is. I'm your big sister." I leaned my head

against the couch, watching my sister, wishing I could make her happier.

Macy toyed with the TV remote. She clicked the TV on and flipped through channels, not stopping on any one show long enough to figure out what it was.

I was tired of feeling bad about stuff. About Audrey, about Gregor. About my parents. I wanted to focus on good things.

"Guess what?" I asked.

"What?"

"I'm going to see if I can get a dog."

"Really?" Macy broke into a huge grin. "A puppy?"

I smiled back at her. "I saw her at the animal shelter this morning. Conner gave me an application, but I need Mom and Dad to agree and then go with me to set up the adoption."

"Conner Lassiter?"

I nodded. "He volunteers at the shelter."

Macy tilted her head at me.

"What?"

"I think you like Conner."

"I do not! We're just friends!"

"You're blushing!" Macy squealed.

"He asked me to Fall Ball," I said once my cheeks cooled off. "As friends." Going to the dance with Conner wouldn't be as romantic as going with Gregor, but it would be fun, I was sure of that. And I wouldn't have to worry what to talk about with Conner.

"Cool! What will you wear?"

"A dress."

"D'oh!" Macy smacked my arm. "You're going to have fun shopping for it!"

"I doubt it will be fun," I said.

"Why? Everything will look good on you."

"Not! Dresses that fit my body are made for ten-year-olds."

"That's not true!"

The front door opened and Dad strode in, his hair rumpled like he'd never combed it this morning.

"Hi, Dad," Macy and I called out.

He stopped and gave us a very sorry excuse for a smile. It broke my heart. He looked miserable.

Macy was either clueless or acted well. "Keiko wants to get a dog! She found one at the shelter. Can we please, *please* get one? Pretty please, Daddy?"

Yeah, great actress that one. She hadn't sounded that young in years. Dad softened immediately.

"A dog?" Dad smiled for real. "That sounds great!"

"Really?" I asked. Could it be that easy? "You and Mom have to be at the appointment tomorrow at the shelter."

"We don't need Mom," Dad said, his voice gruff.

"Actually, both parents have to be there," I said quietly.

Dad didn't answer. Instead, he set his mouth in a straight line and snagged a stack of magazines I was pretty sure Mom hadn't read yet. As he took them outside to the recycling bin, my heart sank. I might get the dog I wanted, but I was pretty sure it wasn't going to fix the problem between my parents.

twenty-three

The rest of the day, I hid in my room, filling out the dog adoption application and researching bichon frises and how to care for shy dogs online. Mom didn't come home until well after dinner, and I didn't bother leaving my room to talk with her.

On Sunday, by the time I went down for breakfast, Mom had already left for work, of course. Macy was at drama practice. Dad walked into the kitchen, newspaper folded under his arm, and poured a cup of coffee. He and Mom used to read the Sunday paper together.

"We're going to the animal shelter when Mom gets home after lunch," Dad said.

"Really?" I hugged my dad. "Thank you!"

He patted my back and then shuffled off to read his paper. If they'd talked about my getting a dog and planned when to go to the shelter, they must have made up. I was still upset with Mom, but I wanted my dog. And I was glad she was finally paying attention to what was going on at home.

I spent the morning doing my neglected homework, knowing there was no way I'd get anything done once I brought my puppy home. I was sitting on the couch reviewing my math homework when the lock on the front door clicked and my mother walked in.

"Hey," I said.

She gasped and touched her throat. "Keiko! You startled me. What are you doing?"

"I live here." The words slipped out before I could stop them.

Mom kicked off her shoes and removed the scarf from her shoulders. "I may not have been around much these past few weeks, but I am still your mother. Watch your tone."

Mom's voice was cross. Something I wasn't used to. I kept my mouth shut but trailed her to the kitchen.

Mom stood at the counter and started straightening her pile of papers and files.

"So, are you ready to go to the shelter now?"

That got her attention off her papers. "What are you talking about?"

"Dad said I could get a dog?"

"He didn't say anything to me about this."

"Well, we're leaving in a bit." My voice hardened. So much for paying attention. If she was home more often, she'd know what was going on.

"I haven't even been consulted about this," Mom said.

I took a breath. "Like you said, I'm having a hard time with my *big transition*. I really need a dog, Mom. She would comfort me and entertain me and keep me company. I'll take care of her. You won't have to help out at all. Macy's excited about a dog, too."

Mom frowned. "It's not that I don't want to help out. I just don't think adding a pet to our household is a good idea right now."

"What difference does it make? It's not like you're home to notice!" The words snapped out of my mouth before I had the chance to hold them in.

Mom's face showed the shock I felt at my unintentional snark. She shook her head once and then stormed up the stairs.

I went back to the couch and flopped onto it. A dog would be there for me. My parents and my best friends were not. I mean, Jenna and I were still friends, but I felt left out and left behind. And I couldn't even think about Audrey without feeling sick. Years of happy memories flooded me—learning how to ride bikes together, swapping our favorite graphic novels, baking cookies at my house, laughing and talking and planning and sharing. Now it was like none of that had ever happened. I really needed this dog more than anything in the world right now.

I stood up when Dad came down the stairs.

"Come on. We're leaving for the shelter now," Dad said.

"Where's Mom?" I asked.

"She's coming."

I felt a mixture of relief and annoyance when Mom slid silently into the front seat. Not one word was spoken during the drive. The silence thundered in my ears. I would have been glad to have Dad turn on the radio and listen to his weird retro stuff at that point.

As Dad put the car into park, I pushed the car door open and walked ahead of my parents to the office. Inside, I gave my name to the receptionist, who showed us to a little room with a desk. The only place for us to sit was on a small bench. Mom and Dad sat on either side of me. I had to get us talking. We had to look like a great family, or the shelter would never let us adopt.

"Thank you for letting me get a dog. I really appreciate it," I told them.

"I think it's good you're showing you're responsible," Dad said.

I opened my mouth to tell him just how responsible I'd be when Mom answered instead. "Are you implying I'm not responsible?"

Uh-oh.

"All I'm saying is that I'm proud of Keiko," Dad said, his voice strained.

No, no, no! I was pretty sure we wouldn't get approved if our family was bickering. Thankfully, my parents stopped when the door opened. In walked a sturdy blond woman wearing khaki shorts and a green T-shirt with the animal shelter's logo on it.

"Hello! I'm Dinah." She sat down behind the little desk. "Keiko?"

I raised my hand.

"Conner is one of our best volunteers. He raves about you." A blush burned my cheeks. "Let me look over your application and ask you a few questions."

My hand trembled as I gave Dinah the paper.

"Fine, fine," she said as she read what I'd written. "Will the dog be left alone for long periods of time?"

I glanced at Mom.

"I'm going back to my regular schedule," Mom said. "I'll be leaving the house after Keiko goes to school and I can swing home on my lunch break."

I was surprised Mom was being supportive. I tried to smile at her. I really did. But something in me held back.

"I get home from school around three," I said to Dinah. "I usually go to the park with Conner to walk his dog."

"Good, good." Dinah looked at my parents. "Will you accept financial and ultimate responsibility for the dog?"

I held my breath.

Both my parents nodded. Dinah smiled and pressed on the intercom and asked for someone to bring my dog.

"I suggest you keep her crated when she's left alone, at least initially," Dinah said. "It helps with housebreaking, although the person who found her said she seemed housebroken."

A girl walked in and placed my dog in my lap. MY DOG. I cradled the white fluffy puppy in my arms. She nuzzled my neck and wagged her tail.

"I think she remembers me," I said. My heart filled up.

Mom leaned over to pet her, but the dog shrank back and trembled.

"What's wrong with her?" Mom asked.

"This dog has had some trauma in her life, we think," Dinah said. "She's extremely timid."

"She is?" Mom straightened. "Is this going to be a problem?"

"She's fine," I said quickly.

"Wouldn't you rather have a friendly dog?" Mom asked.

I glared at Mom. "She is friendly! She loves me." I cuddled the dog closer to me.

Dinah looked unsure.

I turned to Dinah. "I did some research. I'll spend lots of time with her and work on building her trust with me and with others. I won't stress her out, and I'll teach her that she is safe now. I'll keep her crated or supervise her at all times."

Dinah nodded, smiling. "You've done your homework and I don't doubt you will take great care of her, but I do need to make sure your family is also willing to have her be part of your household."

"We are," Dad said.

I nearly slumped to the floor with relief. Mom and Dad paid the adoption fees, and I agreed to use my allowance and do extra chores around the house to pay for the dog license and extras.

We got back in the car, and I held my sweet new friend on my lap. Even with all the tension between my parents, a smile burst on my face.

"Yuki," Mom said from the front seat as Dad pulled out of the parking lot. "I had a white dog named Yuki when I was little."

I never knew Mom had a dog. "Yuki," I said, trying the name out loud. I liked it, but I wasn't about to admit it to Mom. Not when I was mad at her. "What does it mean?"

"It's Japanese for snow."

My hand stilled on my dog's head. Snow. It was the perfect name. I whispered in my dog's ear. "Hi, Yuki."

When we got home, after a quick stop at the pet store for supplies, Dad went straight to the kitchen. Mom followed, asking him what he was doing.

"I'm making dinner. Something you don't do or participate in anymore."

"What's that supposed to mean?"

I stood in the living room, holding Yuki.

"I mean, you're never home. I have to do everything these days. It's almost as if you're not even part of the family anymore!" Dad's voice got louder and louder.

I retreated to my room, saving Yuki from all the yelling. I sat down on my bed with her in my lap. My phone rang and I snatched it, grateful for any distraction from my parents arguing downstairs.

"I hear you're the proud owner of a bichon frise mix," Conner said.

I grinned. "I am!"

"Does she have a name yet?"

"Yuki. It means snow in Japanese," I said.

"Hmm. You have a thing for snow?" Conner asked.

"What do you mean?" I was surprised Conner had noticed.

"You were asking about snow at Doug's."

"Yeah."

"So is there some special thing about snow?"

I curled up on my bed. Yuki tucked herself against my chest. I could feel her little heart beating against me. "My grandpa lived with us for a year before he died," I said.

I paused. I hadn't ever told anyone about Grandpa and how hard he was to be around when he'd moved in with us. Not even Audrey.

"He was grumpy most of the time and didn't talk much," I said, stroking Yuki's head. "But, one time, he told me a story about how Grandma loved the snow."

The memory came back to me as if it were yesterday.

We'd been walking along the beach bike path. It was rare that Grandpa left the house at all, but that afternoon he'd invited me out for a walk. He hadn't been drinking as much when he'd first moved in.

"Grandma loved the snow," Grandpa had said. "One Christmas, I surprised her with a trip to Vermont. We stayed in a rental house in Montpelier. Cute little town where Grandma could poke around in shops. She was so happy all bundled up against the cold. Her cheeks rosy and her eyes bright.

"It had just snowed the night before and it looked like a painting outside our window. Before she even had her morning coffee, Grandma bundled up. She didn't even change out of her PJs. She threw on a thick winter coat, pulled on a knitted cap, wrapped a long scarf around her neck, and tugged on a pair of snow boots. She had left her gloves at home and hadn't yet had a chance to go shopping, so she pulled on my gloves. She clomped through the kitchen and flung open the back door. The crisp, cold air blew in, chilling the small house. Grandma stepped out onto the back porch, holding on to the railing in case it was icy, but it wasn't. It was the perfect snow."

Grandpa turned to me. "Did you know there are different kinds of snow? Sometimes it's wet and heavy, which is good for making snowballs and building snowmen. Sometimes if it's really cold, it just freezes up and it's more ice than snow. But the snow that morning…" Grandpa turned back to face the ocean, and his eyes got that faraway look again. "That snow was perfect. Light and fluffy with only the thinnest layer of ice at the top of it so it crunched when you walked on it. I'd followed Grandma out the door to watch her. She stepped through the fresh powder. Not one print anywhere. She was the first to walk on it. It was still and quiet. No cars or people out yet. No animal sounds. No breeze that made the bare branches creek and moan.

"So there was Grandma, all bundled up, looking like a bear, lumbering down the stairs. Crunch, crunch, crunch. And when she got to the middle of the yard, she turned to face me." Grandpa got quiet for a long time. I stayed very still.

"Oh, Keiko, she was beautiful. Her eyes shining, smiling the biggest grin ever."

I was afraid Grandpa would get sad remembering this about Grandma, but when I peeked up at him, he was smiling.

"Then Grandma fell backward, arms spread out. At

first I thought she slipped, but then she started swishing her arms and legs, making a snow angel." Grandpa laughed. "Just like a little kid, making a snow angel and laughing and laughing."

Grandpa got quiet for a very long time. Then he put his hand on my arm. "Promise me, Keiko, that when you see snow, you'll think of Grandma. I know you don't remember her, and I'm sorry you never really got to know her. She was special in every way. She made me a better person. Grandma is in every snowflake, in every crystal of ice. Grandma *is* the snow."

"I promise, Grandpa," I said, but I wasn't sure he heard me.

The memory faded out like the end of a movie. I rubbed my eyes with my fingers.

"Wow," Conner breathed. "That's a great memory of your grandparents."

We were both quiet for a moment. It was a comfortable silence. I'd stopped petting Yuki, and she nudged my hand, making me smile and breaking the spell.

"That's why I love the snow," I said. "Or why I would if I ever got to see it. It's a nice memory of my grandpa, and while I don't remember my grandma, I think the snow would make me feel close to her, you know?"

"Yeah, I get it."

"Thanks for listening." I couldn't remember the last time I'd talked so much with Conner.

"Anytime," Conner said. "Hey, after our game at the park tomorrow, we could take the dogs for a walk. Sound good?"

I smiled. "Sounds good."

I hung up the phone, and for the first time in a long while, I felt like everything was going to be okay.

twenty-four

Dad honked the horn impatiently, something he never does since it's rude to the neighbors so early in the morning.

"If you want a ride," Mom said, "you'd better get moving."

I nuzzled Yuki one more time. She'd slept with me all night, and I didn't want to leave her.

"Keiko, I've taken care of dogs before. I promise I'll do everything you wrote down." Mom waved the two full pages of notes I'd written up. "I'll take her out right before I leave at eight thirty. And I'll come back at lunch to let her out again."

"Are you sure?" I asked. "I mean, won't you be busy?"

Mom stroked Yuki, who let her. She was already getting used to our family. "I'm finished with the grant, if that's what you mean. I'm back to my regular schedule."

She and I exchanged a long look. Fine. Maybe I could trust her with Yuki, but that didn't mean I forgave her.

Dad honked again.

"Go," Mom said.

I kissed Yuki goodbye and handed her over without saying anything else to my mom.

At school, Jenna gushed as she looked at Yuki's picture on my phone. "She's adorable! You're so lucky!"

Mr. Jay strode into the room, balancing his usual large coffee on a stack of books.

"Do you want to hang out after school?" Jenna whispered. "The paper isn't meeting today."

I nodded, thrilled to have time with Jenna.

When I got to language arts, Audrey wasn't there. Her seat remained empty for the entire class. Not knowing where she was made me squirmy. I ate two squares of chocolate in between classes, but for the first time in a long time, they didn't make me feel better.

At lunch, the guys indulged me and looked at every single one of my fifty-eight pictures of Yuki.

"Jenna's coming over to meet Yuki after school," I said to Conner.

"Cool!" He smiled. "We still on for a walk later, or you want to do it another time?"

"No, Yuki needs a walk. Maybe come over around four?"

"You got it!"

"Wait," Doug said. "No basketball?"

"Sorry," I said. "You'll just have to play without me."

"But Wednesday?" Teddy asked. "You'll play Wednesday? It's been good to play two-on-two."

"I'll be there Wednesday," I promised.

The day was going great until I got to math class.

"You look happy," Gregor said as I sat down in front of him.

"I am," I said.

"We miss you at lunch."

I turned to face him and raised my eyebrows. "*We*? Really?"

"Well, okay, maybe *I* miss you."

My heart did a stupid skip. I turned back around to get my math notes out of my backpack. My fingers skimmed my chocolate bag, but it was empty. Between playing basketball with the guys all last week and getting Yuki, I'd forgotten to restock.

Gregor tapped my arm. "Maybe we can have lunch together tomorrow?"

"What?"

"Lunch? You and me?"

"But what about Audrey?"

"I thought you two were fighting?" he said.

Why did he sound amused? All the stupid giddiness I felt dropped away. "Are you saying you'd have lunch with me and not Audrey?"

"Yes." Gregor laughed. "Are you having trouble with the English language?"

I narrowed my eyes at him. "Are you implying that I can't understand because I'm Asian?"

"Never mind," he said. "Don't get all weird. I was just trying to be friendly."

For the first time ever I was grateful when Nicole and Kimmie slithered into the classroom and wrapped around Gregor. He completely forgot about me, and I was relieved. Why didn't I feel happier that he'd asked me to eat lunch with him?

That thought sat in my stomach like a bad piece of chocolate for the rest of the day.

∾

I told Jenna about Gregor's invitation as we walked to my house. "What do you think that means?" I asked.

"Maybe Gregor and Audrey broke up?"

"So then he asks me out? That seems wrong."

Jenna shrugged. "Maybe they aren't even together?"

"But he asked her to the dance."

"That doesn't necessarily mean they're boyfriend and girlfriend."

Right. Like me and Conner.

"Maybe Gregor likes you?" Jenna said. Then she laughed when I made a face. "Okay, so I guess you don't like him anymore?"

"I don't know. I guess not."

Yuki barked as soon as we walked in the front

door. I hurried to the kitchen, where she was crated. She whined, and her tail wagged furiously.

I opened the crate door, and Yuki dashed out, leaping on my legs. I scooped her up and laughed when she licked my face.

"She's cute," Jenna said.

Yuki turned to Jenna, tucking her ears back and snuggling against me. She trembled. I'd warned Jenna that Yuki was shy. Jenna sat down and I sat next to her, making soothing sounds to Yuki.

Jenna ignored Yuki and said to me, "When's Conner coming over?"

"After they play a game, so maybe in an hour."

"It's nice that you hang out with Conner," Jenna said. "But you can hang out with me and Elliot anytime, too."

"Thanks." It was so weird, all three of us hanging out separately.

We both got quiet. Yuki squirmed out of my arms and stretched her neck out to sniff Jenna, who stayed very still.

"Good girl, Yuki," I said to encourage her.

Yuki stayed in my lap but placed a paw on Jenna's

knee. Jenna put her hand out and Yuki sniffed it. She wagged her tail as Jenna slowly stroked Yuki under the chin, careful not to reach over her head. Jenna and I grinned at each other.

"Hey," I said. "Maybe we should check on Audrey, you know? She wasn't in school, and Gregor was being all flirty with Nicole and Kimmie. Not that that's different from before, but if Gregor and Audrey are together, shouldn't he be less into other girls? Wait, why are you giving me that look?"

"I can't believe you're worried about Audrey after what she did!" Jenna twirled her fingers around Yuki's fur. "What about what Audrey said about not putting guys before friends? Isn't that what she just did?"

"I think I did it first, in her eyes."

"What do you mean?"

"She got mad when she found out I hung out with Conner after school one time. That's when it all started."

"Did you ditch her to hang with him?"

"No. She was busy with Fall Ball committee stuff. Conner invited me to go watch him play basketball."

"How is that putting a guy before her?"

"I knew she hated Conner."

Jenna shook her head. "You're not making any sense. Do you hear what you're saying? Do you really believe all that or are you, as usual, making excuses to keep things conflict-free?"

I shrugged.

"I think you're in denial," Jenna said. "But at least your intentions are good. Still, Audrey dating Gregor was totally wrong."

"I don't care about any of that anymore," I said. "I just want us all to be friends again. Don't you?"

"I don't know."

"Jenna!"

"I'm serious. She's such a drama queen, and she kind of proved to me just what kind of friend she is. I don't miss her."

That broke my heart. "Well, I do. She needs us. Audrey's always been there for us."

Jenna didn't say anything.

"She was there for you during your parents' divorce. She always made sure to have butter-brickle ice cream for you in her freezer. She didn't push you to talk about anything."

Jenna nodded.

"She was happy when we became the threesome we are today."

"No, that was you," Jenna said. "It was obvious she wasn't happy about my joining you guys."

"It took her a while to warm up, but she did."

Jenna nodded again.

"And she cares about me. Like in fourth grade when she arranged for me to work with Conner on our science fair project, because she knew I was interested in the same thing he was."

"You have to reach all the way back to elementary school?"

"No. I'm just saying she's always encouraged me and supported me."

"Fine. But it's usually all about her. As long as things go her way, she's supportive. When they don't, like you and Conner being friends, she gets mad."

"Jenna, she's not all bad."

"You're right, she's not. She's smart and funny and exciting to be around. But she's not a great friend. Not now at least." Jenna stood up and stretched her back. "Why should it always be you who sacrifices? Why can't you do what you want to do for once?"

I scowled. "That's what I'm doing now. I want to make up with Audrey."

"I'm not going to stop you from being friends with her, Keiko. But I don't think I can be friends with her anymore."

That made my heart hurt. "What if she apologized?" I asked, trying not to seem like I was pleading.

Jenna scoffed. "Like that would ever happen."

"But if she did?"

"If she did and she meant it. Maybe."

That was good enough for me. I knew Jenna only wanted what was best for me. She wasn't entirely wrong about Audrey. But I just wasn't ready to give up on my friendship with her.

And I was sure I never would be.

twenty-five

That evening, Macy knocked on my door and poked her head into my room. "Mom wants us downstairs. Now." Macy didn't look particularly optimistic.

I followed her to the kitchen. I did not have a good feeling about whatever was coming.

Mom and Dad were already seated at the table. Dad's face was neutral, and his body language gave nothing away. Macy dropped down into her chair and crossed her arms.

I sat. This had better not be the Divorce Speech. Anger bubbled in me. I glared at Mom, daring her to say something stupid.

"Well," Mom said, resting her arms on the table. "It's been too long since we've sat down as a family."

And there it was. "It sure hasn't been *our* fault," I said.

"So is everyone mad at me?" Mom asked, her shoulders drooping. "Because I've been working?"

"No," I said. "We're not mad because you're working. We're mad because you're never home!"

"That's the same thing," Mom said. "I've been working. We discussed this when I took the promotion. It meant full-time hours. And then writing this grant proposal, which I told you all meant extra hours, was temporary."

"You went out to dinner every night. You go to the bar for drinks. You're going to the spa! You work, but then when you have any free time, you don't spend it with us!" My voice got louder and louder with each word. And it felt like a knife was digging into my heart.

Dad reached over and patted my hand. I wasn't sure if it was to calm me or to let me know he agreed with me.

"I see," Mom said. "I wasn't trying to make you all feel like I didn't want to be home. I'd never written a grant proposal before. I had a lot to learn in a short time. Fortunately, Mrs. Kitamura has experience in writing grants, so she taught me on her own time. We mostly met over dinner since that was when we were both free. We went to the bar the other night to celebrate. And I'm taking her to the spa as a thank-you for all her help."

"You could have said something," Dad said softly. "You could have told us what you were doing."

Mom nodded. "I should have. I was really stressed out and wasn't thinking straight. I'm sorry."

"We missed you," Dad said.

"I missed you guys, too. I'm sorry for making you feel like I didn't care. I was worried I wouldn't be able to do my new job well. I guess that was taking all my energy." Mom's gaze swept the table. "I love all of you. I love my job. That means sometimes I'm not going to be home as often as I'd like. But that doesn't mean I don't care about you."

Dad reached out for Mom's hand. "And we love you."

Mom stretched her hands to the center of the table. Dad kept hold of her hand and squeezed. I slid my hands to the center, and Mom held them in her other hand. We all looked over at Macy. I nudged her with my foot, and she slowly reached out one hand and placed it over all of ours.

~

That night, the four of us made dinner together. Mom and Dad talked and laughed. Yuki scurried underfoot, hoping for dropped pieces of carrots from the salad. Macy smiled for the first time in ages.

We finished all the prep work, and Macy went to let Yuki out while Dad took a phone call in the living room. Mom came over to me where I was setting the table and she took a handful of forks and set them out as I placed the knives. When we were done, Mom pulled out a chair and nodded to me. I sat down and she sat next to me.

"I'm sorry, Keiko," Mom said.

"Yeah, I know. You said that already." I didn't know why my voice was all sullen. I mean, I was happy that everything was okay again.

"No, that was an apology to the family. This is my apology to you."

"What do you mean?"

"You have always been so capable, so reliable, that I sometimes forget that you're still a child." She saw my face and smiled. "Okay, not a child, but not quite an adult. I think Dad and I rely on you too much to take care of things. We sometimes forget that you need us."

"I heard you and Dad once say that you didn't ever have to worry about me and that I did a great job taking care of Macy."

"You did? When?"

"Back when Grandpa lived with us."

Mom nodded. "That was a tough time. And I saw how good you were with Grandpa and with Macy. We should have done a better job of protecting you though. You weren't old enough to be that kind of responsible, especially when Grandpa started drinking."

"He wasn't dangerous," I said.

"No. Just very sad and very angry about Grandma's passing." Mom squeezed my hand. "It was wrong of me to assume you didn't need taking care of, Keiko. I'm here for you, and I'm here for the family. So is Dad. You go have fun and be a kid." I raised my eyebrows at her. "Sorry, an almost teenager."

"What are you saying?"

"I'm saying stop worrying, stop trying to take care of everything. That's my job. I want you to know you can count on me. I'm sorry I haven't been here for you and your sister. You are not responsible for us. You are only responsible for yourself." Mom cocked her head at me. "I know you're going through a tough time with your friends. I'm here if you need to talk, okay?"

"Okay."

Macy came back in, laughing as Yuki nuzzled her. Dad returned to the kitchen, putting his phone in his pocket.

"And you and Dad?" I asked. "You guys are okay?"

"We're definitely okay. We love each other. Sometimes we disagree or argue, but we apologize, we work it out, we forgive. Do you forgive me?"

"I forgive you." I leaned into my mom and we hugged.

As we ate dinner, the four of us with Yuki sitting patiently by my side, I thought about what Mom had said. They'd had a fight. They'd apologized. Everything was okay now.

Hope bubbled up inside me. Suddenly, I knew I could fix Audrey and me.

twenty-six

The next day, I got to language arts as fast as I could.
Audrey's seat was empty. Everything that Mom had
said last night rang in my head. People who love each
other can disagree and fight, but they also forgive
and make up. Now that I knew forgiveness was possible,
I wanted to hurry and get through it. I wanted to be
over our fight and to be best friends again. It was all
a big misunderstanding. We got our feelings hurt,
and we lashed out. We could admit we were wrong
and get back to being friends again. I was always
ready to forgive Audrey, but I think I was afraid she
wouldn't forgive me for being friends with Conner.

But that was silly, right? Our friendship was more important than any of that.

My classmates filed in, and I watched the door, waiting for my best friend.

She never came. Her seat remained empty the entire period. After class, I asked Ms. McQueen where Audrey was.

"She transferred to last period," Ms. McQueen said.

I'd always thought only romantic relationships caused heartbreak. That's how it was in the movies. But no one ever tells you that a friend can break your heart, too.

~

I moped through the whole lunch period.

"What's up with you?" Conner asked as I picked at my sandwich.

"Audrey transferred out of the only class we shared."

Conner reached over into my baggie and ate a couple of my potato chips. Sharing our lunch was new as of yesterday. I liked it. I'd stopped buying food in the cafeteria. Without Jenna or Audrey to eat with, it seemed like a waste of time. Now I packed my own.

"I hate fighting with her," I said.

"Is it because she's dating that Whitman guy?"

I didn't answer and Conner frowned.

"Are we playing basketball today?" I asked.

"We have our three-on-three," Conner said.

"Oh yeah, I forgot."

"You coming?" Teddy asked.

"Of course," I said. "I'll bring Yuki. Do you want me to get Lumpy, too?"

Conner's eyes lit up. "That'd be great! I never have time to get him for the game. Don't be too late though."

"Yeah, you don't want to miss our super moves," Doug said.

I laughed, but on the inside I still felt awful. Especially when I got to math class and Gregor smiled at me.

"Hey. Nice shirt," he said.

I glanced down at my baggy purple T-shirt. Okay. Was he being sarcastic? "Um, thanks?"

He laughed. "You're so sensitive. Lighten up, Carter."

Nicole and Kimmie walked in. Gregor waved at them but kept his attention on me. Nicole glared at me as she sat down. She whispered with Kimmie, and the two of them shot me dirty looks.

"What are you doing after school?" Gregor asked.

"Going to Conner's basketball game," I said.

"Conner? Audrey's idiot brother?"

"He's not so bad," I said.

"Oh, Conner Lassiter?" Kimmie said, interrupting. "He's hot!"

"Totes," Nicole said.

I raised my eyebrows at them. Were they serious? Or just trying to get Gregor's attention? Either way, I didn't like it. They should mind their own business.

I wished Mr. Fordiani would hurry and get to class. He was usually here before any of us. Funny how just a couple of weeks ago I would have been thrilled to be talking with Gregor.

"You could do so much better than that jerk," Gregor said to me, not even acknowledging Nicole or Kimmie.

Gregor had no right to call Conner anything. He didn't know him! As I was struggling for something to say, a youngish, dark-haired man walked into the room and scribbled an assignment on the board. He introduced himself as Mr. Mann, which caused a few giggles, then plopped himself at the desk and put in earbuds. That gave us all pause, but only for a few seconds. We worked on the assignment because we knew Mr. Fordiani would be back and there would be consequences.

A note dropped on my desk.

Ditch Conner and hang out
with me —G

What was Gregor up to? I shoved the note in my bag, refusing to respond.

I wished Mr. Mann would actually do his job and teach a lesson, or at least pay attention to the class. By now the noise in the classroom had grown to a low buzz. But Mr. Mann was fully engrossed in whatever he was listening to.

Gregor tapped my shoulder, and I sighed as I turned to face him.

"We never got to know each other," he said.

This was true. We didn't know each other. Why had I had feelings for him at all? He still had gorgeous eyes and a melty smile, but I felt nothing for him anymore.

Gregor reached over and moved a piece of my hair from my face. I jerked back as if he'd burned me.

He laughed. "Don't look so panicked. Why do I make you nervous?"

"You don't."

"You're cute when you make that face."

How could Gregor be flirting with me if he was with Audrey? Even Audrey deserved better.

For once, the bell was my friend, and it saved me from having to continue to talk with Gregor. I snatched my book and backpack and scrambled out of the room before he could say anything else to me.

Unfortunately, Nicole caught up with me. "Too bad about your friend and Gregor," she said.

"What are you talking about?" I asked as Kimmie flanked me on the other side.

"He broke up with her," Kimmie said. She and Nicole stopped walking, knowing they now had my full attention.

I stood with them next to the water fountain. "How do you know?"

"Gregor asked me to Fall Ball," Nicole said with a smile. "And I said yes, of course."

"Also, he stopped meeting us at the end of lunch

for a while," Kimmie said. "But now he's hanging with us for the entire lunch period."

Nicole and Kimmie smiled at each other and sashayed away.

A chill came over me. Gregor had ditched Audrey. Where had she been spending lunch period? Probably all alone and heartbroken.

After everything—the way she'd frozen me out and gone after Gregor—I still cared about her. She'd been my best friend almost my entire life. That counted for something. And like Mom said, people who love each other can fight and make up. I wasn't going to wait any longer. But first I was going to deal with Gregor.

twenty-seven

As I hurried to PE, I sent a long text to Audrey. I told her I'd heard the horrible news and how sorry I was about Gregor. That she should stop by my house after school so we could talk. I didn't know if she would come over, but I knew she was hurting. She needed her best friend, and I was going to be there for her.

After PE, I caught Jenna in the locker room and told her what happened.

"Well, that's awful," she said, closing her gym locker.

"I'm going to find Gregor," I said.

"And do what?"

"He shouldn't get away with treating Audrey like that!"

"I'll go with you," she said.

"Really?"

"Yeah, really."

"Why are you doing this?" I asked Jenna as we walked across the track back toward the main building. "I thought you hated Audrey."

"Hate is a strong word," Jenna said. "I don't like how Audrey's been acting, but that doesn't mean she deserves to be treated badly. Besides, I've got your back."

"Thanks," I said.

"What about you?" Jenna asked. "Why are *you* doing this?"

"I know you think I'm too forgiving and that I don't stand up for what I want, but this *is* what I want. I want to be friends with you and Audrey. And I'm standing up to Gregor because he hurt her."

"It's a start," Jenna said. "I like seeing you riled up."

I rolled my eyes, and Jenna laughed.

"Look over there," Jenna said.

A small crowd gathered near the side entrance gate,

all girls, except for one familiar face at the center. I marched right up to the group, not even sure if Jenna was still behind me. I pushed my way through the throng right up to Gregor. He grinned at me.

"There's room for all of you. No need to shove, Keiko." His voice, the one that used to make me melt, sounded like it could curdle cream. "Is this your other friend?"

Jenna had kept up and she slid in next to me, her face impassive.

"You're heartless, Gregor Whitman," I said, continuing forward, backing him up against the fence.

The crowd of admirers fell back, but they didn't leave. My face was inches away from Gregor's. He smiled. Why was he smiling? Then I felt his hands on my hips. Our bodies were nearly touching. I gasped and tried to step away, but his hands kept my body in place.

"Let go of me," I hissed.

"You're the one who pressed up against me." He let go and I stepped back. I turned to make sure Jenna was still there. She was. Conner, Doug, and Teddy walked past. I thought to call them over for support, but Gregor interrupted.

"What do you want, Keiko?" Gregor asked.

"You're a selfish jerk!"

Gregor laughed. "Okay."

"Why are you laughing? You treated Audrey like trash when she was nothing but nice to you." I was assuming at least, since I hadn't been there.

"Ah, Keiko to the rescue. Nice."

"This isn't funny."

"Please. You and Audrey are alike. You're both little girls not ready for real relationships. Grow up."

"What is that supposed to mean?"

"It means, I never made any promises to Audrey. She got clingy and possessive."

"So you dumped her?"

"Look, kissing isn't a commitment. Sorry she thought it was. Besides," he said as he waved his hands at the small crowd of girls behind me, "life is short. Why get tied down?"

My heart thumped. He'd kissed Audrey.

"Are you sure this isn't about something else?" Gregor asked.

"Like?"

"You and me?" He took a step toward me, and I

stepped back, nearly tripping on Jenna. "I know you like me, Keiko."

I spluttered. No coherent words came out of my mouth.

"Adorable," he said. "But as much as I think you're cute, you're not ready for me."

I blinked at him.

"It's too bad." Gregor leaned close to me. "I've never kissed an Asian girl."

"What?" The heat that flooded my face had nothing to do with embarrassment for once.

He shrugged. "I've only dated white girls. I'm not opposed to interracial dating. Asian girls are hot."

I couldn't believe what I was hearing.

"The two Asian girls at my old school could hardly speak English. I mean, you're in our country, learn the language! At least *you* don't have a weird accent. But you're half, right? Do you even count as Asian? Whatever! I say half counts!" Gregor laughed.

Oh. My. God. It felt like my head was about to explode. I didn't even have time for rational thought. "You are a first class racist!" I spat.

"I just said I'd date you, so how can I be a racist?

Well, I'd date you if you weren't such a kid. In fact, I'm like the opposite of racist because I *want* to date an Asian!"

"You are insensitive and rude, not to mention totally full of yourself. Saying you want to date me just because I'm Asian, like you have a checklist, does make you a racist! You're the one who needs to grow up," I shouted.

"Thank God I didn't get involved with you," Gregor said. "Too much drama."

"Well, we agree on one thing," I said. "Thank God we didn't get involved!"

Gregor continued smiling, but it wasn't a warm smile.

I grabbed Jenna's arm. "Let's go," I said. "Audrey lucked out by getting rid of him."

"*I* dumped *her!*" Gregor called out after us.

I walked so fast Jenna had to jog to catch up to me.

"That. Was. Awesome!" Jenna shouted.

I slowed down and glanced at her. She was grinning so hard. "How was that awesome?" I asked.

"You!" Jenna said, laughing. "*You* were awesome!"

"Stop," I said. "I was not. I lost my temper. I ranted."

"You lost your temper. Congratulations. You're human after all."

"God, I can't believe his stupid comments. 'Does half count?' What a jerk!"

"You rock!" Jenna bumped shoulders with me.

"Thanks," I said without much conviction.

"Seriously, Keiko," Jenna said. "I'm proud of you."

It did feel good to say how I felt, even if I had lost my temper. I allowed myself to feel some pride, which was new for me. I kind of liked it! It gave me a boost of confidence for what I needed to do next.

"I texted Audrey to meet me at my house," I said. "You coming?"

Jenna's smile faded. "What are you going to say to her?"

"I want us to make up. I want us to be friends again, like we used to be."

"I don't think we can ever go back to how we were," Jenna said. "I'm not going to stop you, Keiko, but I'm not ready to forgive her. She needs to apologize first."

"But that's the whole point. How can she apologize if we don't give her the chance?"

Jenna shook her head. "It's not like she doesn't know how to find us."

"So you're really not coming?" I couldn't believe this.

"I'll tell you what. If Audrey really is sorry and apologizes to you, then I'll consider talking to her." Jenna shrugged.

When Jenna and I split off at the corner, I stopped for a moment and watched her walk away. Her hair sparkled purple in the sunlight. She turned and waved at me, and I waved back, even though my stomach was clenching. This felt so wrong.

But I could fix it. I would make up with Audrey. Audrey would make up with Jenna.

And then everything would be perfect again.

twenty-eight

When I got home, Yuki greeted me at the door. I swooped down to pick her up. Macy was sitting in the kitchen doing her homework.

"Thanks for letting Yuki out," I said.

"No problem." Macy leaned back. "Oh, Conner came by."

"I forgot! I was supposed to bring the dogs to the park for his game. Was he upset?"

"I don't think so." Macy stood up. "I'm going to Claire's. She's helping me run lines. I'll be back by dinner."

I didn't ask any prying questions. Mom said to let go

and that I didn't have to be in charge of everyone and everything. It was hard, but I was trying.

As soon as Macy left, I took out my phone and dashed a text to Conner, apologizing for bailing. I waited a few minutes, but when he didn't respond, I figured he was out with the guys. It had only been one afternoon, but already I missed him.

A knock at the door made my heart trip. I was torn between wanting it to be Conner and wanting it to be Audrey. I knew it wouldn't be both. Would Audrey actually show up?

"Come in!" I called out, and I held my breath in anticipation.

Audrey walked in and I grinned. She'd read my text! She'd come over! It had been way too long since she'd been here. I held Yuki in my arms and stood.

Audrey halted. "You got a dog?" she asked, not moving a muscle.

I nodded, wondering if she'd treat Yuki like she treated Lumpy. If so, I already knew who I'd choose if she said it was her or my dog.

Audrey inched her way into the room and sat at the

very edge of Dad's recliner like she was about to bolt from the house.

"Her name is Yuki. She can be shy," I said. "So don't make any sudden moves. Let her check you out."

I set Yuki down, and she slowly stepped over to Audrey's feet. She was getting much better with new people. Yuki sniffed Audrey, and her tail wagged.

Audrey reached out to touch Yuki's head, but Yuki backed up and barked. Audrey flinched like Yuki had tried to bite her. Realization struck me like lightning. Audrey would have appreciated the cliché, but now wasn't the time. "You're afraid of dogs?" I asked, scooping Yuki up in my arms.

She scowled at me. "You just now figured that out?"

I sat down and held Yuki on my lap. "I thought you just hated Lumpy, you know, because of Conner."

Audrey tugged at her shirt.

"How could you not say anything?"

"Conner would have used it against me. He probably would have trained Lumpy to scare me on purpose."

"He wouldn't have done that."

"Whatever. That was a long time ago," Audrey said. "He treats me like garbage."

"Maybe you and Conner can stop fighting," I said. "Maybe if you apologize and explain why you were so mean to Lumpy."

"Right. And then he could apologize for being a jerk. And then we'll hold hands and skip over the rainbow."

Yuki was extra sensitive to tone, and she trembled in my arms. I released her, and she dashed up the stairs to my room.

I took a deep breath, the kind Audrey used to tell me to take when I got wound up. This was not the way I'd envisioned our reunion. "Gregor is an idiot," I said.

Audrey's glare disappeared, and tears pooled in her eyes. "Are you going to gloat?" she asked, her voice trembling.

"Of course not!" I sat down on the couch across from her. "I told him off after school!"

"You did?"

"Yeah," I said, smiling. "Jenna came with me. He can't get away with hurting our best friend!"

"You mean that?" Audrey wiped the tears from her face.

"You're better off without him," I said as I handed her the box of tissues from the coffee table. She grabbed a handful and swiped her face.

"I know, but it still hurts." Audrey sniffled and played with her tear-soaked tissues. It reminded me of the failed sleepover at her house. She had been crying then, too. Audrey had been through a lot since school started.

"Maybe we can start fresh," I said. "You, me, and Jenna."

"Maybe."

That gave me hope. "Look, the three of us have been friends for a long time. Jenna didn't intentionally get together with Elliot to hurt you, just like I know you didn't get together with Gregor to hurt me. We shouldn't let guys come between us."

"You mean that?" Audrey looked at me.

"Of course. Our friendship is the most important thing of all."

"Then forget about Conner," Audrey said. "Let's work on fixing our friendship. We can't do that if you and my disgusting brother are hanging out."

"Audrey," I said.

"You're the one who said it, Keiko. Don't let guys

come between us," Audrey said. "I missed you, Keiko. We need our girlfriends. Boys come and go, but friendship is forever."

My head was muddled. I'd told Conner that I could be friends with both of them. I didn't want to give up Conner for Audrey, but I wanted Audrey back.

Suddenly, Audrey crumpled. She put her head in her hands, and her shoulders shook.

"Audrey!" I leapt up and rushed over to her. I squeezed in next to her on my dad's chair and wrapped an arm around her.

She sobbed and sniffled, then grabbed more tissues.

"God, it just hurts so much." Audrey rocked back and forth, tears streaming down her face. "I really, really liked Gregor, you know?"

"I'm sorry he hurt you, but I'm glad he's gone. You deserve someone way better!"

Audrey dabbed her eyes. "I told myself I wouldn't do this, get all emotional." She took three deep yoga breaths. "Our friendship is the most important thing of all. Look at what Gregor did to us. It's a good lesson learned."

I nodded, cautiously, not sure where she was going with this. I scooted back onto the couch.

"I really want to get our friendship back on track. Jenna and Elliot are going to the dance. They're a couple. Fine. But you and Conner, it's not like you're in a real relationship. I know he's just using you to get at me."

"No, Audrey, he isn't using me. We're friends. And we're going to the dance with Jenna and Elliot."

Audrey looked shattered. "You're going to the dance? With my brother?"

I realized I was grasping my hands together. Tightly. I forced myself to loosen my grip.

"Well," Audrey said, flipping her hair over her shoulder. "You don't want to waste going to your first dance with a friend. Wait till you have a real boyfriend."

A real boyfriend. I liked Conner. A lot. I liked him more than I thought I ever could. I looked forward to being with him. I had fun with him. But were we more than friends? Probably not.

Audrey wiped her face with a tissue. "Don't go, Keiko. It would kill me, sitting at home all by myself while you and Jenna were at the dance."

I sat back against the couch. Audrey held her wet tissue to her face, waiting for my answer. Her eyes were red and swollen, and she really was heartbroken.

Friendship meant sacrifices and compromises. Maybe Conner would be okay with not going to the dance. It's not as if Audrey were asking me not to talk to Conner or be friends with him. She was just asking me not to go to the dance. I could do that for her.

"Sure," I said with a heavy heart. "What are friends for?"

Audrey flung herself at me and squeezed me in a tight hug. I hugged her back. I knew I should be happy to have my best friend back, but instead all I wanted to do was run upstairs and be with Yuki.

twenty-nine

The next day, I had lunch with Audrey for the first time in forever. While she talked about the outfit she was planning on buying at the mall that weekend, I wondered what the guys were doing. I texted Conner to let him know I had made up with Audrey, but he continued to ignore me. I had to prove to him that I could stay friends with him, too.

After school, I went to my locker, but Conner wasn't there. I waited for five long minutes, but I knew he wasn't coming. He was always there first, waiting for me. I grabbed my backpack, not bothering to put my books in it, and hurried to his locker, the weight of the books pressing against my achy chest.

Was he avoiding me on purpose? I glanced at my phone to see if he'd texted me back. I scrolled and saw nothing but old messages. Why was he doing this? He knew that I wanted to be friends with Audrey again. Now that she and I were finally good, he was ignoring me! Thinking about Audrey reminded me that I'd told her I wouldn't go to the dance with Conner. I slowed down, suddenly in less of a rush to find him. My steps felt as heavy as my heart. Why was everything so hard?

When I made it to Conner's locker, all three of the guys were there. They turned to watch me approach. Conner's face was grim.

"Hey," I said when I reached them. "Sorry about missing lunch."

"And our game," Conner said.

"Right, and your game, too."

"Don't you want to know who won?" Conner asked.

Doug and Teddy both shifted back and forth on their feet, like they were itching to run. I kind of felt the same.

"Who won?" I set my bag on the ground, still holding

my books in my arms. Conner didn't answer. "Conner," I said. "Don't be mad about Audrey. You know I wanted to make up with her."

Conner raised his left eyebrow. Something he did only when he was annoyed.

Silence dropped like a brick. I distracted myself by taking that moment to put my books into my bag. Anything was better than just standing there. I fumbled my books and dropped one onto my toe. I cursed. Something I never do.

Conner squatted down and picked up my book, handing it to me.

"Thanks." I tried to shove the book into my bag, but it wouldn't go. I cursed again.

"Keiko," Conner said. "Calm down."

How could I be calm when he was the one acting all weird? Conner reached over and took the book out of my hand.

"Here, just take everything out and you can make your books fit," Conner said in a voice like I was a skittish stray.

I dumped my backpack upside down, notebooks and books thunking onto the ground. A piece of paper fluttered out, caught in the breeze, and skimmed across the walkway. Teddy chased after it and handed it back to me, but I was busy stuffing my books back into my bag. Conner took it.

"We're out of here," Conner said, standing abruptly. He shoved the piece of paper into my hand. "Don't lose that. I'm sure it's special."

I glanced down at the paper. It was Gregor's stupid note from math, telling me to ditch Conner and hang with him. Why had I kept it?

I grabbed my things and ran after the guys.

"Conner! Wait!"

He kept walking, but Doug and Teddy stopped. I ran past them, grateful that I wouldn't have to explain everything to Conner in front of them.

I caught up to him just past the school gates. "Slow down," I gasped. "I want to talk to you."

Conner wouldn't look at me, but at least he slowed down enough for me to walk next to him. I struggled to find the right words to say while trying to catch my breath.

"Fine," Conner said. "Let's get this over with. I'll make it easy on you. You want to break up, right?"

I stumbled over my feet. What? I didn't even know we were together. "What are you talking about?"

Conner stopped, looking at me like I'd lost my mind. "The note from Gregor!"

"It's not what you think."

"And how do you know what I think?"

"You're mad at me, you're ignoring me. At first I thought it was that I was friends with Audrey again—"

"That's part of it," Conner said. "Already you're ditching me for her."

"God! It shouldn't have to be a choice!"

"You're right. It shouldn't be, but Audrey always makes it one," he said. "And you always choose Audrey."

"I'm trying my best here. Audrey and I have been friends forever. I want to be friends with both of you. I don't want to break up. That is if we're together," I said. "But can we not go to the dance?"

I pushed the words out in a rush, getting them out of the way.

"Oh. I get it." Conner started walking again, more like jogging. I had to run to catch up. I grabbed his arm, but he pulled it from my grasp.

"Conner! Wait! Don't be mad," I shouted as he kept fast-walking away from me.

He stopped two houses away and turned to face me.

"You can't have everything, Cake!" His voice smacked hard against my nickname. "You can't be with me while you wait for Gregor to ask you to the dance. I saw you with him after school, standing close together!"

"Conner, no!" My stomach churned. This was not going at all how I'd wanted.

He shook his head, looking more sad than angry. "If that's what you wanted, why didn't you say so? Just be honest."

"That's not it at all. I don't like Gregor!"

"No? Then why don't you want to go to the dance with me anymore?"

I took a step toward Conner, and he took a step away from me. So I stopped. But he kept walking backward, like he couldn't get away from me fast enough.

"Because of Audrey!" I shouted.

"Great!" Conner said in a tight voice. "You said you could be friends with Audrey and me, but it's obvious you can't. You'll choose Audrey every time, even though she treats you like dirt. If that's what you really want, fine! I just want you to be happy. Don't you?"

My throat closed up as he turned the corner and disappeared. I wrapped my arms around myself. Once again, I thought I'd gotten what I wanted, but I'd lost something in the process. Conner's question needed to be answered. Didn't I want to be happy?

Something had to change. And maybe that something was me.

Thirty

When I got home, Yuki greeted me so enthusiastically that I couldn't help but smile. I clipped the leash on her collar and headed back outside. My shadow stretched across the browning lawn as shadow Yuki trotted ahead.

Frustration spread through me. I walked faster, my feet matching the speed of my whirling thoughts. How could Conner accuse me of wanting to go to the dance with Gregor? Never mind that maybe he got the wrong idea from seeing me with Gregor after school. And from reading that note. And me telling him I didn't want to go to the dance anymore with him.

"Gah!" I shouted at the sky.

Yuki stopped walking and looked at me, her ears tucked back and her stubby tail between her legs.

"Sorry!" I scooped her up and she nuzzled my neck. I hugged her to me. "I'm messing everything up, Yuki."

My thoughts spun and congealed, and I couldn't seem to focus on any one thing as I put Yuki back down and started walking again. Well, that wasn't quite true. I was thinking of Conner, but I was so confused. Why did I care so much that he was mad at me? Now I could just go back to how things were before, when Conner and I weren't friends and I was BFFs with Audrey.

She and I had made up. This was what I'd been working toward. Soon we'd be meeting at the library after school and hanging out and going shopping like we used to. But all I could think about were the things I'd be missing. Lunches with Conner, playing basketball, walking the dogs, laughing at his silly jokes. His easy smile and floppy hair. Oh, and movie night at Doug's. It was my turn to choose a movie. I was pretty sure I wasn't invited anymore.

Yuki yipped and tugged on her leash, pulling me out

of my thoughts. I'd ended up at the park. In the distance, the rhythm of a dribbling basketball beat out a comforting tempo. It was calling to me.

Just then, Conner shouted in triumph as he made a basket. His voice echoed in my head. My breath caught like I was plunging off a cliff, and my heart started to slam against my chest.

Oh my God. I liked Conner. I mean, *like*-liked him. The realization filled me with a mixture of joy and fear. Mostly joy. I think.

I already really missed him. I wanted to keep hanging out with him every day. No matter how I felt about him, I knew one thing for sure. He had been a good friend.

If not for Conner, I wouldn't have Yuki. And Conner had figured out I had a thing for snow. That phone call when I'd told Conner about Grandpa, he hadn't interrupted once, or tried to change the subject, or talked about himself.

Even in the heat of our argument, Conner had said he wanted me to be happy. He'd stepped aside so I could be friends with Audrey. He would do that for me. Because he understood that it was nearly impossible for me to put my own happiness first. Why? Why did I do that?

And then it hit me. I thought that if I didn't make sure everyone was happy, then maybe they wouldn't love me anymore. By taking care of everything, I was important. Needed. But Mom said I didn't have to do that. It wasn't my job. And deep down, I knew she was right. Mom, Dad, Macy—they loved me. I didn't have to do everything for them. I could just be me. It should be the same with my friends.

The thought of telling Audrey how I really felt scared me. But I couldn't blame her for not being sensitive to my feelings if I never shared them. If she truly cared about me, she would want me to be happy.

I started running home, and Yuki scampered to keep up, her tongue out, her tail high. I was suddenly filled with excitement and hope that I was finally going to get what I wanted. All I had to do was speak up!

Thirty-one

I dropped Yuki off at home and then texted Audrey to let her know I was coming over.

"Hi!" Audrey squealed fifteen minutes later, and tugged me into the house. "We have the place all to ourselves!"

I followed her into the den, where she sat on the couch and started rummaging through one of the many bags on the floor. She'd gone shopping.

"So?" Audrey asked. "Did you talk to him?" Her voice seemed full of giddy anticipation.

I knew she was asking if I'd told Conner I wasn't going to the dance. I hadn't thought it would be hard—Conner was usually pretty easygoing—so I'd been totally caught off guard when he'd gotten upset. Telling Audrey that I wanted to be friends with both her and Conner was definitely going to be even harder.

So I stalled, walking over to the shelves and perusing the familiar framed pictures. Something seemed different. A new small brass oval frame was tucked to one side of Conner's shelf. I leaned closer. It was a picture of me. My breath hitched as I picked it up.

"He pulled it out of our family album a couple of weeks ago," Audrey said, sounding put out. "Mom yelled at him because now there's an empty space on one of the pages."

The picture was from the summer. Mr. and Mrs. Lassiter had had a delivery in Santa Monica for a celebrity client. They wouldn't tell us who, but the house had been huge, behind stone walls and an iron gate. Audrey and I'd had to wait in the car, but nobody recognizable had come to the door. After that, Audrey's parents took us to the pier for games and food.

The photo Conner framed was a candid one Mr. Lassiter had taken of me standing at the railing, gazing at the ocean. My hair was in a ponytail, but a few wisps of hair had slipped out and fluttered across my cheek in the breeze. It was my favorite photo of me ever, but I'd been too shy to ask for a copy.

I put the frame back on the shelf. It was a wonder Conner hadn't tossed it out the window by now.

"You done staring at yourself?" Audrey snapped.

"Why are you so against me and Conner?"

"Because you know how I feel about him!" Audrey pulled out a pink sweater from one of her bags and smoothed it over her lap.

"That's between you two. He hasn't done anything to you that you haven't done back to him."

Audrey pouted and refolded the sweater. "It doesn't matter," she said. "You don't need him. You have me again. We're starting fresh."

But the thing was, I did need him. He was the one I wanted to talk to about things like Grandpa and Yuki. He understood me. Did Audrey even get me anymore? Did she care?

When was the last time Audrey had done something nice for me? I paused. Actually, when had I done that for Conner? My heart sank as I realized that all this time, I'd taken him for granted. He was there for me, and when it counted, I hadn't been there for him. Shame washed over me. How was I any better than Audrey?

She made a sound, and I realized I hadn't responded to her. The silence had drawn out for so long that I couldn't remember what she'd asked me.

Audrey gripped the sweater on her lap. "Conner isn't your friend. I am."

"I want to be friends with both of you."

Audrey threw her sweater back into the bag. The paper rattled loudly, making me flinch.

I took a big breath. "Things have to change, Audrey. Conner's been a good friend to me."

"You are deluded," Audrey said, mostly under her breath but loud enough for me to hear.

"I do want us to have a fresh start. So let's do that. Things can be better even if they're different."

"What exactly are you saying?" Audrey narrowed her eyes at me.

"I'm saying that I want to be friends with both you and Conner. That's the way it has to be."

"Is that an order?" Audrey sneered.

I shook my head. "No. You have a choice. You always have a choice."

Audrey blinked, like she was seeing me for the first time. And maybe she was. Maybe now she could see how important this was to me.

"You're right," she said. "We always have a choice. We've been best friends forever, Keiko. We have history. You don't have anything with Conner, except whatever you've been doing with that weirdo the last few weeks."

My heart sank. Audrey wasn't budging. And she was never going to. "So you're saying I have to pick one of you?"

"I'm saying you have to pick me!"

I turned to look at my picture sitting on Conner's shelf. All my true happy moments these past few weeks had been with him. If I reached back further, before the name-calling, Conner and I had always had fun together.

How could I choose Audrey?

How could I not choose Conner?

The choice was clear, but that didn't mean the decision was easy. And there would be fallout.

"Oh, Audrey," I said softly, facing her. "I can't do things just to make you happy anymore. I mean, I do want you to be happy, but not if it means I have to be unhappy."

"What are you saying?" Audrey stood up.

"Do you remember at the start of summer, you told me that I should go after my own happiness?"

Audrey crossed her arms.

"I want to stay friends with you, but I also want to be with Conner."

"You're an idiot," Audrey said. "You always act like you care about everyone else, but you only care about yourself."

Right.

"I have to go find Conner," I said. "I need to apologize to him."

"Apologize to Conner?" Audrey shrieked. "What about me?"

"I'm sorry, Audrey. I really am." I walked to the door, Audrey trailing me.

"You're seriously going to throw away our friendship? Over Conner?"

I reached for the doorknob. "I never threw away our friendship." That was the truth. "I like Conner. He makes me laugh, and I feel happy around him." It felt good to admit a truth, to claim it. "I can't fix everything. I can't make everyone happy. It's not my job."

"You're horrible at it anyway!" Audrey's voice was brittle. "If you walk out that door, we're through. If you go to the dance with Conner, you and I can't be friends. Ever. It's not like I need you. I have new friends. But you'll need me, eventually. Do this, and I'll never forgive you."

"There's no way we can compromise?" I asked, knowing her answer. No more making excuses for Audrey. It wasn't like this made me happy. It wasn't like I didn't want to stay friends, but it was obvious now that we couldn't. "Goodbye, Audrey."

Thirty-two

I went back to the park, but by the time I reached the basketball courts, Conner and the guys had left. I glanced at the time on my phone. Since Conner hadn't come home, he was most likely at Doug's by now. There was no way I wanted to have this conversation with an audience.

I called him but got sent so quickly to voice mail that I knew he had seen my number and declined. I stared down at my phone, blinking back tears. I didn't really blame him. Of course he was still upset, but I didn't want to drag this out any longer.

"Text message it is," I said to myself as I walked home. I composed a million of them in my head, but nothing seemed right. I knew I only had one shot. Conner would most likely ignore my text, but if he glanced at the first line, I wanted to make it count.

I dashed up the stairs to my room, Yuki bounding after me. We sat on my bed. Having her curl up against me gave me dash of comfort and a shot of courage. I had to send this before the guys started watching their movie.

"Here goes nothing," I said to Yuki.

I choose you, Conner. I told Audrey. I know you're mad at me, and I don't blame you. But even if you never talk to me again, I still choose you.

My heart was in my throat. Or maybe it was in my stomach, because I kind of felt like I was going to be sick. I stared at my screen for the longest ten minutes of my life, willing it to change from "delivered" to "read." Maybe Conner was already watching a movie. Or maybe he really didn't want anything to do with me. I leaned my forehead against my knees, feeling like the world was ending.

"What are you doing?"

I startled and straightened as Macy poked her head

into my room. I tucked my phone back into my pocket. "Nothing. What's up?"

"Mom and Dad want to play Boggle," Macy said with a grin.

"Right now?" I had been so focused on my phone that I hadn't heard everyone come home.

Macy nodded. "They're ordering pizza for dinner."

I smiled. I was glad for a distraction. I didn't want to think about Conner ignoring my text. Plus it had been a very long time since we'd had family game night. I cradled Yuki in my arms and followed Macy downstairs.

Mom and Dad had already set up the game on the kitchen table. I slid into my seat as Macy placed a bowl of chips on the table, and Mom handed me a chocolate bar from a company I'd never heard of.

"I saw this at the grocery store and thought you'd like to try it," Mom said.

"Thanks!" My mouth watered. I couldn't remember the last time I'd had any chocolate, which was weird. I unwrapped it and took a big bite as Dad passed out the notepads and pencils. The chocolate was bittersweet but balanced, and the texture smooth. Maybe that's what our family was now, balanced and smooth.

My thoughts wandered to Conner. What kind of chocolate was he? And for that matter, what kind was I? I'd never really thought about it before. And that's when it hit me. Conner and I were like my spicy hot chocolate. The ingredients didn't seem like they'd go together, but they did. And not everyone liked the blend. It was unique, special, and appreciated by only a few. Too bad Conner and I would never be.

"That was a big sigh," Dad said to me. "Already gearing up to lose?"

"Ha-ha," I said, snagging a pencil. "Let's go!"

Mom put the Boggle grid down with the letter cubes in place, and we all started writing, the only sound the scratching of pencils on paper. The first word I saw was LOVE, and then BALL, and then DOG. I blinked. I needed more challenging words.

"Time!" Macy called when three minutes were up.

We played several more rounds, until Mom won with fifty points. When it was finally closer to dinnertime, Dad ordered the pizza and I set up the grid for another round while we waited. We'd just started when the doorbell rang.

"That's awfully fast," Dad said.

"Well, you did complain to them last time that they took too long," Mom reminded him.

"I'll get it," I said, "but don't play without me."

I grabbed the change off the table and went to open the door. But it wasn't the pizza.

It was Conner. My heart stuttered. Conner was standing on my porch. His chestnut hair was smoothed back. He wore Adidas sweatpants and a gray hoodie I'd never seen before.

Yuki barked and jumped on Conner. He knelt down and stroked her head, smiling down at her. I wished he was smiling that smile at me.

"What are you doing here?" I asked, keeping my voice neutral.

He stood. "Can we go for a walk?"

"Let me ask," I said, about to head to the kitchen.

"Go ahead! We'll play without you!" Mom called.

Just as well that we were leaving, since my family was eavesdropping. I slid on my shoes. Conner held the door open for me as we stepped into the evening.

"So..." Conner said. We headed away from my house, down the block.

"So." My voice came out shaky. I tried to take a calming breath, but it didn't help. I was full of nerves. Cool air brushed against my skin, and the rustle of leaves in the trees reverberated in my ears. Even our footsteps, evenly matched, sounded loud on the pavement as we walked.

Why was Conner here? I couldn't stand the suspense and I didn't want to walk in a silence that was so full of questions.

"Where are we going?" I asked instead of the real question that was on my mind.

"The bubble tea place?"

"Oh. I haven't been there yet. Is it good?"

"I don't know. But I remember you telling Audrey you wanted to go this summer."

"You heard that?"

"Yeah, and that she didn't want to go, even though you wanted to."

We walked half a block more, my thoughts running in a loop. If he was taking me to the bubble tea place, he couldn't be that angry, right? *Speak up, Keiko,* I thought to myself.

"Are you still mad at me?"

Conner glanced sideways in my direction, but he didn't smile. We both stopped walking.

"I have to give you something." Conner pulled out a metal box from behind his back and handed it to me.

"What's this?" I asked.

"Open it."

I held the square box, the cold metal chilling my hands.

"Hurry," Conner said.

"Why?"

"Just open it. Now."

That Conner looked so nervous made *me* nervous. "It had better not be one of those coiled-up toy snakes that jump out at you."

Conner reached over, opened the lid, and dumped the contents into my hands. It was cold. And wet.

"A snowball?" I asked as I realized what I held. "Where did you get a snowball in October, in Pacific Vista?"

I cupped my palms around it, compressing the ice into a compact ball. The chill pricked at my skin.

"It's the best I could do," Conner said. "I grated ice cubes. My mom caught me, and now she probably thinks I'm totally strange."

"You made me a snowball?" The ice melted quickly in my hands, cold water dripping through my fingers.

"Do you like it?"

"I love it," I breathed. "It's the most wonderful thing anyone has ever done for me."

Conner's smile warmed me from head to toe.

"Thank you," I said, looking down at the melting snowball and then back at Conner. Those eyes. That smile. "So you're not mad at me anymore?"

"I got your text."

"Oh."

"*That* was the most wonderful thing you've ever done for me," Conner said.

"I haven't really done much of anything for you," I said reluctantly. "You've been this really great friend to me, and I haven't appreciated you. I'm sorry."

Conner smiled at me, and my heart did a jittery jumpy thing.

"I'm sorry I got all weird and jealous over Gregor," Conner said. "I believe you that there wasn't anything going on."

I breathed a sigh of relief.

"And I'm sorry Audrey made you choose, but I'm not

sorry you chose me." Conner reached out and took my hand.

"I do choose you, Conner Lassiter," I said softly.

Conner grasped both my wet hands, and my heart hammered.

"Keiko, just so we're clear, will you be my girlfriend?"

Conner was adorable when he blushed. I hoped my blush was just as adorable to him. I could barely catch my breath as I said, "Yes."

"Um." Conner's face remained bright red.

"What?"

He leaned toward me, and I didn't pull away. I just closed my eyes as his lips pressed against mine, a little rough but warm, and I kissed back. When we pulled apart, we both grinned. My first thought was that I couldn't wait to tell Jenna. But then I thought, *Why am I thinking about Jenna?* Conner kissed me! And he was still standing right in front of me.

I was going to take charge of my own happiness, starting now. So I rose onto my tiptoes and put my lips on Conner's for my second kiss. It was even better than the first.

acknowledgments

It takes approximately four hundred cocoa beans to make one pound of chocolate. While writing a novel is a solitary endeavor, it takes many people to bring it to a delicious finished product. I have no doubt that at least four hundred people influenced or helped me on my way to publication, and I appreciate every single one of them. Special shout-outs to the following:

For helping make my dreams come true, my agent and my editor. Many thanks to my agent, Tricia Lawrence, for believing in me and my writing. Your guidance and friendship mean the world to me. Deep gratitude to my editor, Jenne Abramowitz, for loving Keiko and her story. Your sharp insight was vital in making Keiko's story shine.

Love and appreciation to Jo Knowles and Cindy Faughnan, my writing partners for fifteen years. You were there the moment Keiko and her friends walked onto the page, and you helped me through many drafts. I am eternally grateful you both changed your writing times when I moved to China, so that we could work together virtually online. Without you and without that, this story and others might not exist.

For helpful feedback, Kristy Boyce, Debby Garfinkle, and Grace Kendall (for the awesome title, too). For making me dig deeper, my amazing mentor Jennifer Jacobson and the rest of the Highlights Foundation Whole Novel Workshop leaders: Melissa Wyatt, Rob Costello, Nicole Valentine, Nancy Werlin, Amanda Jenkins, and Sarah Aronson. A special thank-you to Andrea Wang for insight, support, encouragement, and, most of all, an everlasting friendship.

The writing road has been long and bumpy. Many friends have encouraged, taught, and guided me. I truly appreciate every one of you. Key people who were very important on this journey: Cynthia Leitich Smith (my mentor at the very beginning), Laurie Halse Anderson, Jerry Spinelli, Jennifer Groff, Daphne Benedis-Grab, Cynthia Lord, Nancy Castaldo, and the LiveJournal writing community from yesteryear. Cheers to the loudest cheerleaders: Kristy Boyce (you deserve many mentions!), Jason Gallaher, Kara LaReau, Ann Braden (for that last crucial nudge), my EMLA family, Elly Swartz, and lifelong friend Lisa Fung. I am especially thankful to my anam cara, Lynn Bauer—my light in the dark, my rock in the storm.

Special mentions: Ben Bauer and Leigh Bauer for answering my questions about teen-related stuff; Jeannine Atkins and Peter Laird for use of their lovely home; cover model Halina James for perfectly embodying Keiko; Dom Ramsey, author of *Chocolate*, for the spiced cacao drink recipe Keiko uses; Corrie Wang for the food truck name; my husband, Bob, for making me a snowball using a grater and ice cubes; and my daughter, Caitlin, for conversations on everything.

To everyone at Scholastic for their tremendous support, including Shelly Romero, Abby McAden, David Levithan, Jordana Kulak, Rachel Feld, Julia Eisler, Lizette Serrano, Emily Heddleson, Danielle Yadao, Stephanie Yang, Yaffa Jaskoll, Josh Berlowitz, Elizabeth Whiting, Nikki Mutch, and the rest of the sales team.

To my mom, Yasuko Hirokane Fordiani, who saved all my writing starting from when I was six years old, took me to the library and never said no to a book I wanted, and hand-sells my books to everyone she knows. I love you. To my late father, Denta Hirokane, who fostered my love of books by reading to me early on—I love and miss you.

I'm lucky to have family who believes in me. Many thanks and love to my stepfather, Bob Fordiani; my sister, Gail Hirokane; my brother-in-law, John Parkison; my niece, Laurel Parkison; and all my aunts, uncles, and cousins. Thank you to the entire Florence family, who welcomed me with open arms—too many to list here—but in particular to my father-in-law, Will; his wife, Irene; and my late mother-in-law, Nell.

To SCBWI for conferences and the writing friends I have today. To teachers and librarians, and authors and illustrators: You inspire me. To We Need Diverse Books for all the important work you do. To my readers and to bookstores, especially Bank Square Books and Savoy Bookshop & Café, thank you for all the support.

I've saved the best for last. So much gratitude goes to my husband, Bob Florence, for years of believing in me even when I didn't believe in myself. You never wavered in your support for me, and you never questioned the money and time I spent on writing. Thanks for listening to me go on and on about my characters, for celebrating with me, and for cooking delicious meals. I don't think I remember how to cook anymore. And thank you for the Word Nest, my writing studio that overlooks a pond. There is no way I could have done this without your love and support.

To Jason Florence—thank you for being a wonderful stepson, for coming to my book signing when I was in your town, and for donuts and hikes and chats about dogs. I'm so happy to have you in my life.

To Caitlin Masako Schumacher for being an amazing and inspirational daughter. For pointing out when you were eight years old that I got blue/crabby whenever I went a few days without writing, for giving me time and space to write and not making me feel guilty, for being truly happy and excited when I got good news, and for always being on my side. Thank you for believing in me. I am the luckiest mom.

Bob, Jason, Caitlin—you are the perfect ingredients for a family. I love you!

about the author

Debbi Michiko Florence is the author of the Jasmine Toguchi chapter books (JLG selections, the Amelia Bloomer and CCBC Choices lists, and a Cybils Award winner). A third-generation Japanese American, Debbi was born and raised in California. She is the proud mom of a daughter, a rescue dog, two ducks, and a rabbit. A former zoo educator, Debbi writes books in her writing studio, the Word Nest, in Connecticut, where she lives with her husband. She, of course, loves all chocolate but favors dark, no nuts, and caramel and maple flavors. You can always find her at debbimichikoflorence.com